Schoolhouse Man

W.F. Ranew

Island Oaks Publishing

Chapter 1 - The School

Riverton, Georgia, 1988-89

Brooks Sheffield felt the tingly sensation of a sneeze coming as he held the musty leather volume. Dust particles covered old banker boxes and floated through the heavy, hot air of the attic room where he rummaged for memories. He sniffled, but no sneeze yet. He set the yearbook on a box, wiped his hand across the mold and thick crust of dust, and studied the front.

The cover read: "Panther Paw. Riverton High School, 1963."

A part of his past, Brooks knew, lay before him. He flipped through the first pages. One by one, those times unfolded, and every mental image of that past spawned a dozen more through faces, events and feelings, some wonderful and others disturbing.

His hand moved back to the inside page, and he looked over the faces in the pictures. Most were smiling. A few, primarily the principal and coaches, looked serious, tough and disciplined. Brooks kept turning the pages, searching for nothing in particular but taking in something from each page. There was danger here, and while he turned casually he knew he would rather avoid parts of the book. His fingers and eyes moved gingerly, seeking the good times and fond memories.

"The French Club -- 'Liberté, Egalité, Fraternité,'" the caption read. The club's members, nine of them, joked and laughed as they stared into the camera. Monsieur John Wesley Pendergast, the school's French instructor and club sponsor, stood tall behind the group. His broad jaws held a plain, flat smile, his hair was cut close and he wore a three-button tweed jacket too short for his frame. His white button-down shirt was closed with a thin black tie loosely knotted and shoved in a cocky, deliberate way under one side of the collar. Brooks mused over this photo.

His nose itched as the allergic reaction to the dust grew. He grabbed a handkerchief from his hip pocket. Unfolding the soft cotton, he placed it over his nose as he sneezed.

This was a special photo. On the back row, standing three places from Mr. Pendergast, was a young man with dark hair as short as the teacher's and with moppy bang falling across his brow. And like his teacher's, the student's smile was flat, although he couldn't hide the inside joke the teacher had cracked just as the camera captured the picture. This boy was chubby in the face, and as much as he tried he failed to conceal the wry smile that wrinkled upward in each corner of his mouth and lit up his cheeks. The boy, too, had on a tweed jacket, but his tie was neatly knotted in a four-in-hand firmly centered in his collar. Brooks Sheffield smiled at this image of his younger self.

He moved a hand to his face with thirty years of age to it since the yearbook picture was made. He had changed some, but his features remained essentially the same. His face felt leaner now, worn from sorrow and pain and, no doubt, from the bottles of whiskey poured down his throat. His jaws sagged slightly and would sag more except for their tightening and thrusting forward, as was his nervous habit, particularly around strangers or in a new situation. His hair now sported a similar tight cut as in the photograph, a sharp taper in the back, neatly squared sideburns and the distinction of gray peppering his head. Still his dark brown hair held some of its youth, despite the gray and the receding hairline now moving towards a widow's peak much like his father had. His eyes were his father's, too. Brooks' eyes gave him away, always, Jane had said. Those big brown, wide-open eyes illuminating whatever emotion moved in him. The eyes, capped by dark, slender eyebrows, were bright and sometimes innocent. They had suffered nothing of his pain, except that they, like his small, thin-lipped mouth, didn't smile as much any more, and they sank often, sometimes from the burden of life and other times by too much drink. A two-day beard now covered his face and his dimpled chin. While he needed to shave, his past came first.

Several pages over Brooks found his likeness again, in the debate team picture. Some of the boys in this picture were also in the French club photo. Their hero, Mr. Pendergast, again stood erect behind these forensic scholars. The caption identified each member, but made no note of the name the all-male team privately called itself, The Master Debaters.

The facing page displayed the full thighs and bare shoulders of cheerleaders, their poses struck in various ways in a montage of photos, some with arms extended upward as eight young girls simulated a cheer, another with the girls jumping, kicking their saddle oxfords nearly out of sight behind them, their skirts flying up around their waists. A picture across the bottom of the page showed one girl, the team captain, spreading legs wide on the grass while the other cheerleaders leaned over her. Smiling, they all seemed self-assured in their youthful sexuality.

The next pages showed the sports teams, then the band and a final spread on the majorettes, who wore far less than the cheerleaders. Brooks reflected on how many of these fresh-faced, innocent majorettes – at least three he could remember -- had dropped out of school after becoming pregnant. He thought, too, that this had never happened to any cheerleaders.

The last pages were left to the advertisers and various candid pictures snapped during school events such as homecoming, the junior-senior prom and graduation.

On a focused search now, he turned back through the pages until he found what he wanted. There she was, Jane Hudson, standing smartly on the back row. The schoolgirl and then the woman he had known better than any other person.

Seeing Jane there sliced through Brooks Sheffield's life. In the picture, she was young and shapely, her cashmere sweater pronouncing her developed teenage body. A string of white pearls, borrowed from her mother, hung around a neck so white and tender. Her blonde hair fell around square shoulders. She was beaming, always. She smiled without hesitation, Brooks thought. There never was any pretense about Jane Hudson. He saw her hands clasped in front of her plaid skirt. Her left hand was bare of jewelry, but one day he would place a diamond ring and gold band on it. Jane Hudson was her natural, beautiful self in this picture. Over the years, her features had matured and yet, years later in the darkness of their lives, she still looked much the same as in this picture, even on the day she died.

Still holding the handkerchief, he wiped tears from his eyes. The danger encountered, the sadness stirred, Brooks closed the book and put it back into the dusty box. He would have plenty of days like this one to rummage through the attic. It was his now. He had moved in to the building at the end of Webster Street. He had a new home in Graystone High School. He was confident the rediscovered memories would never again fade, and he held no thought that one day soon they might die altogether, forever.

After deciding to move into the school building, Brooks Sheffield's only quandary was where he would live inside the large, old structure. He had justified keeping the building -- which passed to him when his father died -- largely by the possibility for living quarters and of leasing some of the space for offices. Neither living quarters nor income drew him to the school, which was in remarkably good repair despite its age and several years of little use. The reason he moved in, the real reason, was his fascination and affection for the gray brick building. He had grown up nearby, watched his cousins attend, and graduated from high school there himself. He loved the building. Now, it was his.

Called Graystone High by the locals, although little granite and other stones were used in construction, for it was red brick painted gray, the building was to have been torn down for a new school. However, the location wasn't right, so the school board approached Brooks' father, who owned other property suitable for the new school. He gave the school board the property in exchange for Graystone High. His father had plans to renovate the building, but the elder Sheffield's health began to fail. Alas, the school and other property around town acquired over the years by his grandfather and father had grown into a collection of old buildings in disrepair and several open city lots covered with debris and dog fennel. Brooks, as his father must have at one time, saw a promising enterprise in the old school, and he planned to turn it into rentable space for law offices, perhaps a kindergarten, maybe even one of Jimmy Carter's foundations seeking to improve the lot of rural poor.

With the schoolhouse, Brooks also owned its several acres of land, an old shop that sat behind the school and a field house next to the football field. The school board still used part of the school and the other buildings for storage and office space.

Of course, Brooks' living in the school and doing something with the building stirred talk all over town. The recent activity befuddled some, but most people were excited about the building's revitalization. Talk spread about the man from Atlanta who had wonderful plans for the old school. He immediately gained the sobriquet, bestowed by the children in his new neighborhood, of Schoolhouse Man, who would make the aging structure into a showplace, one Chamber of Commerce official said.

"Heard he was going to set up a trade school out there," said Wallace Harris, proprietor of Harris Co. Seed & Feed, one morning over coffee at the Regal Cafe. The other regulars had their own opinions about Brooks Sheffield and his old schoolhouse.

"Trade school, my ass," said J.D. Riley, a retired businessman from Atlanta who had moved to Riverton several years ago and immediately took on the mannerisms of the country. "School board know 'bout that? And what's he going to teach -- loafin'?"

"That boy's not hitting on but about five cylinders. I can

tell you that, 'cause that old place ain't worth a dime. Hell, it's falling down," offered Tommy Simpson, who owned a farm but made his living driving a school bus.

Brooks didn't move as fast as people's expectations and imaginations. He took his time with his plans. So in a few weeks, when no carpenters and masons and plumbers had assaulted the schoolhouse with their tools, people began wondering whether this man, Brooks Sheffield, native son and all, had any plans at all for the schoolhouse. Some whispered the man was off his rocker, which clinically could have held some truth to it, Brooks supposed in a light moment of considering all the money he had spent on psychotherapy in Atlanta. Other people just figured he was taking his time, and they were mostly correct. Eventually, people dropped the talk of Brooks Sheffield, regarding him silently as a man disturbed, or, in kinder words, a lonely native son who had come home to rest, worn from city life and the terrible loss of his spouse.

As moving day approached, Brooks still had not decided where he would live in the building. He had spent several days walking the halls, each time intending to choose the space for his apartment, but instead he spent his time wandering, remembering and pilfering small items here and there, from the basement science lab and the girls' restrooms to the second-floor storage areas behind the small auditorium. At the end of each day he was no closer to choosing his quarters than when he entered.

The science lab smelled the same, like a science lab. Dust was everywhere. Although a few empty jugs and jars littered the room, nothing else remained of chemical lab equipment. Absent were glass beakers and rods, rubber hoses and brown bottles in the cabinets. Still, the acrid smell of chemicals pervaded the room. He picked up a small brass valve attached to a rotting rubber hose on the floor and stuck it in his pocket. He also admired some of the large, open-mouth glass jars, thinking he could use these for the pennies, dimes and nickels he collected. In the girls' restroom at the opposite side of the basement from the science lab, he found several bars of soap and packs of paper towels. He took a handful of each for use later. On the second floor, he opened the door of the teacher's lounge storage room to find cartons labeled "sanitary napkins" stacked nearly to the ceiling. In the auditorium, he spent at least an hour digging through boxes of musty, tattered costumes and a collection of old stage props. The largest of these was a set of three pastoral landscapes reminiscent of paintings by William Turner or John Constable, so fragile now that his hand punctured the rotted canvas as he moved it to view the next. He left the sets alone, but he found an ancient navy blue baseball cap with a fading "R" across the front. He slapped the cap against his thigh several times, donned it, and headed downstairs. After all this, he felt his sneezes return and he went out to his car for a box of tissue and an antihistamine.

Finally at week's end, Brooks moved into the basement because it was the most convenient place to set up house and one room's window air-conditioner worked. He chose an end room, one with its own access to the outside and one near a restroom with showers. Years ago a gymnasium had stood just outside his corner basement window. The gym, which folks in Riverton called a "shell," had burned down. Now, looking out the south wall of windows Brooks had a view of the street through hedges planted in the gym's ashes.

Brooks had envisioned his basement room as temporary until he could build an apartment in the attic, his choice for permanent quarters. The school's attic had been seldom used. Now, it was dusty and kept a few boxes of school records, library books and old yearbooks along with discarded roofing tiles and tar. Its space was vast, though its ceiling at eight feet was lower than those in the rest of the building. The attic's arched window provided ample light, was well above the street lamps and, more importantly, afforded a wonderful view of Riverton. From this window, which easily cleared the branches of a live oak, Brooks could see the west face of the courthouse clock, sun glinting off its housing during the day and, at night, its face glowing hour by hour across the small town.

The problem with the attic room was its lack of plumbing. The only bathrooms with showers were in the basement. In the end, the attic became a forgotten dream. The basement room was practical and accessible to everything he needed, so he stayed there.

After a couple of months, Brooks began to settle in with the school's hollowness, its night noises and its mysteries. Despite its physical expanse, the school building was becoming as familiar as any living area, as comfortable as any home.

It was in the attic that Brooks discovered the treasure box of Riverton history in old yearbooks, which extended his view of the past to years before he was born. And it was to this upper room that he retreated, many times at night, to think and watch the passing moments of the small silent town that he often thought was fading, perhaps dying, down below him.

The building, seventy-five years old, served as the high school for the town's white residents until it was abandoned for a new structure in the early 1980s. Its construction had begun in 1912, and the school opened for classes in fall of 1913. At the time, the building represented a culmination of the town's leap forward in education for its white residents. Riverton's blacks struggled with shabby education for decades after that, but for the white folks, the sparkling new three-story gray structure was symbolic of rebirth, of growth, of development in the years since the War Between the States. To them, the school promised prosperity in those early years of a newborn century.

For the people of Riverton, this new high school also represented an elevation in social and cultural standing. It meant a proud showplace of modern science laboratories, expansive classroom space, a comprehensive plan of study from one grade to another, built-in plumbing and restrooms and, the greatest attribute for the town's arts matrons, a stage and music rooms. A story and editorial in The Riverton Herald's edition of September 19, 1913 sang the new school's praises:

NEW RIVERTON HIGH SCHOOL OPENS
FOR FIRST CLASSES NEXT WEEK
Public Invited to Opening Ceremonies;
School Officials Call New Building 'Resplendent'

All of Riverton will be proud to see the opening of the new high school, which is located in the western part of town at Lauren and Webster Streets. The new building features modern classrooms and equipment.

Of brick construction, the school is three stories tall and shines brightly with light gray paint accented with white on the cornices and columns. The Doric columns reach from the first story entrance on up over the second story. The magnificent front entrance beckons visitors up grand steps and into a foyer outside the administration offices of the superintendent of schools and the principal.

The first floor features eight classrooms, the library and the school administration offices. The second floor houses four other classrooms, a teachers lounge and auditorium, which seats 624 people and whose stage will be lighted often for dramatic, music and other presentations. The school's basement is equipped with classrooms to be fitted out for the science laboratories.

Another amazing feature is the school's gymnasium with shower areas for both boy and girl students. Various school activities will be centered in this area, which is in the basement underneath the first floor library.

Superintendent Giles cordially invites the public to opening ceremonies at nine o'clock in the auditorium.

Editorials
RIVERTON ENTERS BRIGHT ERA IN EDUCATION
AND CULTURE AS NEW HIGH SCHOOL OPENS

A grand day approaches with the opening next week of Riverton's long anticipated new school. Superintendent Giles of the City Schools reports the school will open for fall classes next Wednesday. The event, however, marks much more than the advent of another year of school or even the culmination of the building's construction. For all of Riverton, this marks the beginning of a higher level of education than ever before seen in the city. The building offers the modern conveniences of the 20th Century along with the promise of the cultural enrichment Riverton children deserve as they grow as the future leaders of our town, our state and our nation.

The school is a great achievement, and we praise those who worked so hard to plan, fund and build it. Your great works will be viewed by a proud Riverton, Georgia, next Wednesday morning.

The passing years satisfied many early expectations. During those years, the school's literary and music events prospered and brought recognition to the faculty, students and their parents. Eventually, Riverton High was awarded state honors for its debate team, one-act play and for its band and choral programs. Growing, too, was interest in football, a sport that Riverton enthusiastically embraced, although without much success in competition.

But it was the school's new gymnasium, built in the late 1920s, and success on its courts that excited and instilled pride in the community year after year. This gym replaced the one built inside the original building. By the late 1930s, games played in the new gym put Riverton on the high school sports map with several regional championships and three state titles, two years captured by both boys' and girls' teams.

Riverton became basketball city, all else taking a social back seat between the season's start in November and March, when the state tournament was held.

The gym became the arena of doom for visiting teams. Built with a limited budget as the town and nation entered the Depression, the gym stood as a dubious memorial to grand sports achievement. The shell was built to be purely functional, with little room for showers and changing rooms. In fact, the shower and locker rooms beneath the bleachers were so small that visiting teams either used the field house -- an uncomfortable place during winter months because the field house's heating system was so frail -- or the showers in the basement restrooms of the old gym in the school.

The shell's seating was simple, too, and reached around three sides of the open room that served as a basketball court, a dance floor for sock hops and a physical education area for those days too rainy or cold to exercise outdoors. The seats themselves were only wide steps of boards worn to a smooth finish by successive coats of gray paint and by the smoothing effect of several generations of use.

By the 1940s, people said the shell's odor had become its most offensive characteristic and its major flaw. The smell emanated from years of sweaty towels and sports garments -- jock straps, shorts, brassieres, panties, T-shirts and socks -- piled unwashed for days on locker room floors. The towels and socks were the worst, as Brooks had witnessed. He and Verny Waters were the trainers for the boys basketball team in the late 1950s. And on the night Riverton's boys won the district championship, all the players changed quickly after the game and headed off to the teen club, a beer hall or to woods and fields to celebrate with their girl. Mounds of clothes were thrown and scattered or piled into the corners. Brooks and Verny celebrated too, in their own way, with neither a cheerleader nor girlfriend in their arms. Brooks and Verny went home and had hot chocolate. Then they went to

bed. The next morning they returned to the shell to gather
and wash the messy, smelly clothing from the night before.

"This is awful," Verny said. The sight, of course, was
disheartening but couldn't compare to the smell. "Jeez, it
stinks. Get me out of here."

Brooks didn't like the smell, either. He just stared.

"How are we ever going to get all this stuff clean,"
Verny whined. "Look, here's Carly Pidcock's jersey. He
looks like he comed on it. Shit, it's gooey and smells a whole
lot worse than B.O."

"Carly smells pretty bad most of the time, Verny,"
Brooks said.

"Yeah, but nobody can smell like this. Not on the
outside, anyway."

After agonizing over the scene a few minutes, both boys
started gathering the clothes. Everything had to be piled into
laundry bags, and taken into the school and up to the washer
and dryer in the home economics classroom on the second
floor. The clothes were nearly gathered when Verny
disappeared.

"Brooks," Verny called from the other side of the shell.
He had been dragging bags of the dirty laundry to the door
when he sidetracked into the girls' locker room.

"Where the heck are you, Waters?" Brooks called. "Get
your butt back in here, and let's get this stuff washed."

"No, come here," was the hollow call.

Brooks moaned and went to find Verny. He walked out
onto the basketball court.

"Where are you, anyway?"

"Down here."

Brooks could tell now what Verny was up to, or at least
why he might be going through the girls' locker room.
Brooks stepped down the stairway and into the room. Verny
was there, reading something.

"What are you doing, here? The girls have to clean up
their own mess. If Coach Mims or Mr. Ryder catches us in
here, going through girls' private lockers, we're dead."

Verny said nothing to that. He just read on.

Brooks looked around. The locker room was just like the boys in most respects. The smell was the same, save an occasional whiff of perfume. For the most part, the smell, the terrible rank body odor, was all over the shell. He walked down to the restroom area and checked out the sanitary napkin dispenser. Nearly full. He checked the trashcan. Tissue smudged with makeup filled the basket and tumbled onto the floor. Wonder when they'll clean this up, he thought.

"Look here, listen to this," Verny said.

"What is it?"

"I found it on the floor. It must have fallen out of her locker."

"Whose?"

"Just listen. 'Dearest Reston...'"

"Is that from Julie Brasington?"

"Yeah, 'Juju,' to us guys who know her intimately," Verny said, letting out a big laugh and poking Brooks in the side.

"Read it, pig butt."

"'Dearest Reston. I just wanted to thank you for the other night. Wonderful! You're divine. The sweater feels warm. I have it on as I am writing this letter. I just got out of a bath and I thought of you the whole time! That's silly, I know. But I thought you should know, too, since I am going steady with you now. You ought to know everything about me, shouldn't you? (And don't think I shouldn't know everything about you, too!) So, I'll tell you more!'"

"What crap!" Brooks said. "Put it back and let's get out of here, Verny."

"Just wait. I'm getting to the good part." Brooks looked over Verny's shoulder to the page with lavish swirls of the girl's handwriting.

"'So I'll tell you more! (Girlfriends can't tell their steadies too much, can they? Don't answer that!) The sweater's warm because that's the only thing to keep me warm. (Oops, too forward am I?) Yep, that's it. C'est la vie, as the French say. It's warm against my body and it makes certain parts of my skin tingle. (Don't say which part, don't you dare! But you know!) It reminds me so much of you because it is you. You tackled all those boys last year for this sweater... for me! And it's for nobody else. You told me it's just for me. No one else has worn this sweater except me. And you, of course. Oh, a scare. Mother just knocked on the door and I had to put on my bathrobe. But now she's gone and the robe is off. And the only thing I have on now, the absolutely only thing is your sweater. And something else you don't know. It's unbuttoned... all the way down, that's halfway to my knees. I like wearing the sweater this way because I not only think of you... I'm with you, and I'm close to you even though you're not here. Just like the other night, after the game against Cairo and we were driving home and we stopped at that little roadside park near Thomasville. I felt so close to you after that. You feel so good to me. And afterward, you gave me this sweater and the next night this big hunk of a ring. Oh forgot? I lied. I'm wearing the ring, too! On the gold chain around my neck. It's dangling close to my heart and my...(!) Reston, love me forever! Don't let me go and don't ever leave me alone. I feel so close to you now. Until tonight when I'll hold you again and again and again and...'"

The agains trailed off the page and dripped over onto the back. Finally, at the bottom of the back of the fourth page, she signed the letter, and Verny read this aloud, too, "Forever and ever, I'll love you. Juju."

Verny looked up: "He screwed her, all right."

"Yeah," Brooks said. "He always brags about getting girls in the back seat of his car, but Juju's not trashy like the girls he usually goes out with. A little crazy, but not trashy."

"Well, that depends on how you look at it, I guess."

"Put that letter back. She hasn't even given it to him yet and you've already wrinkled it and messed it up with your sweaty hands."

"Oh, gosh! You're right. The FBI will be here tonight

taking fingerprints. Put it back! Put it back now!" Verny's dramatics were wearing thin.

"Shut up. Let's get out of here," Brooks said. But Verny wasn't ready to leave just yet. He wanted to continue looking around, and after placing the letter back on the floor, he proceeded to do just that.

"Just a minute. Let's poke around over here a minute. This is our big chance, Brooks."

So Brooks followed as Verny pawed through the small lockers.

"Look at this, here's Wanda Smith's locker. And look at this bra, it's full of Kleenex! I thought she had truly big tits."

"Oh hell, she does," Brooks countered, examining the bra Verny held high. "Those are just to round her out."

"Well, it looks like cheating stuff to me."

Brooks opened a locker and looked through the contents. A home economics textbook and several notebooks rested unevenly on clothes and tennis shoes. A note was taped to the back wall of the locker. "Keep your hands off! Unless you want to tangle with Tiger Annie!!!" It was Annie Chambers' locker. Annie was a big, athletic girl who played every sport in the school except football. She would have participated heartily, and surely with great success, on the gridiron, too, were she allowed on the team. In fact, she did play a mean game of touch football. Because of this, her size and her speed, in particular, touch football teams always chose her first, sometimes before choosing some of the boys.

She acquired the name "Tiger Annie" because of her regular participation in athletic activities. She was tough, aggressive and known to growl during grab fights for the basketball. In these, Annie always won, either by gaining possession of the ball or being called for a foul, which she relished almost as much as getting the ball. Riverton Junior High teams, where Annie had first crowned her reputation in official regulation play, were called the Tigers. The name stuck, even in high school where the team name was the Panthers. Besides, "Panther Annie" just didn't have the same punch to it.

Her locker told the story of her life and bespoke her dominion over the playing field. Oversized tennis shoes, a huge bra, T-shirts larger than any of the other girls, socks the size of a linebacker's, a varsity sweater of similar proportions and a box of super-size sanitary napkins. Annie was big, and in the parlance of those who observe big people often and who distinguish carefully among all types of size and the reasons for hugeness, Annie had not an ounce of fat on her. She was big, and in a strange way had a big kind of beauty, but her manner and style were often cross and demeaning. She rarely smiled unless she was mocking, teasing or bullying someone. Although Annie was neither a natural nor constant bully, she could jump on girls and boys alike if she thought they were making fun of her. That was Annie's point of sure-fire response to being made fun of, ridiculed or slighted. Of course, no person of sound mind in the school would ever tease Annie to her face. Nobody was that stupid. Plenty of people laughed at her, though, people too small in mind or maturity to recognize Annie's skill in sports. When Annie thought she someone was laughing at her, she moved quickly and directly on the culprit and proffered an appropriate punishment.

That's why Brooks was confused when he picked up a pair of Annie's panties. Her panties, a clean pair of which were also in the locker, felt as dainty and silky as any of the other girls' underwear. And they had a fragrance, not of perfume, but a clean, nice smell. Brooks ventured so far as to point this out to Verny.

"Look here," Brooks called to Verny. He pointed out the bigness of Annie's things and yet how her panties seemed small, in fact too small and too lacy for a girl who wore blue jeans and the most plain of dresses and who felt comfortable in gym shorts or gray sweat clothes most of the time. Verny stared at Brooks for a moment, puzzled.

"You moron," Verny said. "What makes you think those

are Annie's panties, anyway? She's the biggest dyke in school and she ain't the only one. Those are probably not hers, they're probably a trophy!"

Verny felt he was very funny, and he laughed and screamed at his little joke on the naive Brooks.

"You ought to know enough about dykes by now," Verny said. "Hell you live on the same street as Annie."

"Aw, I hardly know her. She's never around, anyway. Never see her."

"Yeah, but you wished you could, right, Brooks? Maybe you two should get together. Maybe she would let you wear her varsity sweater! You could wear it in the raw, Brooks. And all the time you could have that 'tingly' feeling your skin gets when she puts it to you, however she puts it too you."

"OK. OK. Enough, someone's going to hear you Verny, so shut up."

Verny's laughter went on and on, and he wouldn't let up on the joking.

"Can you imagine cuddling up in the back seat of a car with Tiger Annie? She'd tear you apart if you tried anything, and if you didn't she'd eat you alive! If she liked you she would give you her sweater, or rather, her tent! It would be a little big, but it would definitely keep you warm... and tingly!"

"I'm getting out of here," Brooks said as he took the panties from Verny, threw them back into Annie's locker and shut the door. He walked past Verny, who was convulsed in his own humor, and headed out of the locker room to wait for Verny.

"Let's go to work, butt hole," Brooks said as he left. Verny laughed and poked around some more, his laughter at first trailing off to chuckling, then to a bored whistling. "Ooo-wee, that Charlotte Templeton really does have great knockers. Not one Kleenex anywhere near her locker. This is a keeper." Eventually, Verny had seen enough of the mysteries within the girls locker room, he settled down from his hysterical laughter and he went back to hauling the full bags of laundry to the schoolhouse, with his treasure from Charlotte Templeton's locker tucked into the front of his blue jeans.

Verny kept the brassiere. Years later, when the gymnasium burned down, he wrote Brooks a letter bragging about his bounty from that cold winter's morning in the gym. In the letter, he told Brooks he was having the bra bronzed, framed and mounted on the wall of his den with the title, "These Once Held Two of the Grandest Ever at Riverton High School."

The night sounds in the old school building occasionally woke Brooks during his first months in his new home. He often heard noises from his basement apartment, and while he couldn't detect the source of some of the sounds, they all seemed nonthreatening: birds flying into windowpanes, squirrels scurrying through the kitchen and lunchrooms or trapped in an endless maze of heat ducts. He remembered stories about the Graystone ghost, supposedly the spirit of a local person who hanged himself in the schoolhouse years ago, no one could ever pinpoint the date.

The building itself seemed a spirit at rest after death, taking a reprieve from a busy life, a hectic life, one filled with the aspirations -- and disappointments -- of so many students, teachers and parents. Tonight, the Graystone spirit slept. Brooks felt its stirring, however, every day when he explored the building and reopened another chapter to its past.

Often he heard human sounds outside, groups of boys walking past late at night, talking, screaming and throwing rocks at the old school, occasionally walking up to the school and shaking the doors, perhaps trying to break into the building. One November night around eleven, he heard a car drive up to the north side of the school near the tennis courts. He walked down the hall and looked out. The car's engine was running and the lights were shining into the northwest entrance to the building. A figure, a man, was facing the northwest entrance steps, where stairs led to the basement on one side and up to the first floor on the other. Brooks listened to the trickling sound of urine splattering on leaves while the man urinated long and steady. Then the car horn beeped. The man turned around and, his job finally finished, zipped up and returned to the car. A woman laughed. The doors were locked.

"Damned it. Open the door."

"Don't you have the key?" was the woman's coy, muffled reply.

"Open the door."

The woman obliged and the man got in, slamming the door. He cut the engine and turned out the lights. The mercury lamp at one corner of the tennis courts lighted the playground and one side of the car, but Brooks couldn't make out the faces of its occupants. For several minutes, no sound came from the two in the car.

Brooks moved closer to the window and looked out. He was too low in the basement to see anything, but he assumed the two were making out. He walked up to the first floor and into the library, where north windows overlooked the playground where the car was parked. Now Brooks was looking straight down on the car. Too high, now, he thought. He walked back around to a classroom, whose windows afforded a view down on the car but at an angle that allowed one to see inside the vehicle. The light from the mercury lamp, filtered only by the outer limbs and leaves of an oak tree, was perfect.

He saw slight movement in the car, the kind of movement lovers make embracing; the man's hand moved slowly and purposely, from the grasp of his lover's hand up to her face. The embrace quickened after she turned sideways into the seat to face him. Heads twisted slightly in a long, heavy kiss. He moved to her neck and gnawed there for just a moment, then back to her mouth. His hand moved again, this time to gently stroke her blouse then squeezing. With this, her right knee moved across his right leg. More heavy kissing, then up for air. She turned around to rest on his lap, again facing him with her legs stretched out along the front seat. Some more kissing as he unbuttoned her blouse, folded it back and nibbled her breasts. Slowly and with some effort they crawled into the back seat. The car started a steady rocking, back and forth.

Brooks left the scene at this point and returned to his basement room. The school was quiet now. He went to sleep before hearing the car leave. No other sounds disturbed him that night. Not that night, and not for some nights to come.

Chapter 2 - Dead

Brooks walked silently and slowly down the second-floor hallway. Other footsteps approached up the stairs, tramping toward the first floor, possibly the second. He heard a voice.

"What we doing here?"

No one replied. The intruders just kept walking up the steps at a steady pace.

On the first floor, they stopped and waited a moment. Brooks ducked into the auditorium, sliding quietly behind loose, dusty and moldy sets, and ignoring the room's chill. The footsteps started again, on up to the second floor. There the steady pace stopped, and the men -- he thought there were two of them -- stood somewhere near the end of the hall and talked. One was nervous and moved around a lot, stepping to a window, Brooks figured, then down the hall a ways, then back. The other man was at ease, in control of the situation, and he had grabbed something to sit on, probably one of the paint buckets stacked at the end of the hall.

"You went to this school, didn't you Louie?" Footsteps moved toward the man who was sitting.

"Yessir, guess about everybody in Riverton went to this school one time or another. Who we waiting for, Boss?"

No answer to the question. Louie didn't press it. He just walked some more. Whose voice was that? Brooks couldn't tell, but he could have known the man, years ago.

"Shore is dark up here. Kinda cold, too."

"Yes, Louie, we all went here. One time or another," the voice finally said. "Myself, I haven't been in this building in ten, twelve years. Keys work though. Ten, twelve years."

Louie was tiring of the unanswered questions, but he tried again.

"What in hell's goin' down?"

No answer.

"This school building must be seventy-five, eighty years old, Louie. Taught most people in town something." A pause. "Me, I learned very little here. You know, Louie, I used to be some kind of athlete at this school. Remember the gym?"

Louie paused before answering. He might have been pondering the question.

"Yeah, yeah, I do," Louie said. "Yeah, sure, the old one that burned down a few years back."

The other man chuckled.

"No, no, son. That was the new gym. Hell, they didn't even build that until I was about out of school. I'm talking about the gym downstairs, on the bottom floor. In the basement."

"Didn't know about that one."

"No. No. You probably wouldn't have, Louie. You probably wouldn't have."

Louie slowed his pace and walked around the hall.

"I was the Big Man back then, back in 1929, '30 and '31. The Big Man. In football and basketball. 'Course, we didn't play other towns when I first started playing, Louie. That was later. When I was playing it was just us boys. Riverton boys, all of us. We played in the local leagues. Churches. Some of the county schools. But that was it.

"That's when I learned a basic lesson, Louie. You play hard enough and long enough and mean enough, and you can beat the livin' shit out of anybody. Big Man. Louie. That's what this school taught me. How to be the Big Man." He paused, cleared his throat. "Tell me, son, what did it teach you?"

"Well, hell, I don't know. Arithmetic, I guess, adding and subtracting. Some multiplying and dividing. I learnt most of what I needed to know at the pool hall. Nothing else worth the time."

"How about the alma mater, Louie, remember that? The song, man, the school song?"

"No, don't think so."

"Well, Louie, I remember it. It didn't change until a few years ago, when the Africans started going to school here. But for a long time, the song was the same:

"Hail to thee, our Alma Mater, hail, hail, all hail. Through the years, we uphold your honor, ne-ver to fail. Hail to thee, Oh River-ton, here we raise our song: Justice, might, hold strong to right, to Ol' Riverton High our all."

Both men were silent. Then Louie picked up his walking pace again.

"Hey, is somebody else s'posed to be here? I understood you to say..."

The old man's voice changed, and fell into gruffness, a mumbling almost unheard.

"Hell, Louie. You know why we're here. Why are we here, Louie?"

"Well, I guess something's happening. I don't know."

"You know what the problem is, don't you, Louie? Surely you learned that much in this old schoolhouse."

Brooks had trouble hearing then. Apparently the other man had gotten up and moved closer to Louie. Brooks couldn't understand the mumbling.

The man rested an arm across Louie's shoulder and drew him near. Then he talked in low, slow tones directly into Louie's ear. Brooks still couldn't hear. The man said: "It's right there in the alma mater, Louie. That's the one thing you should have listened to all the times you heard it sung. Not that you would ever sing something like that, something meaningful and right. This school. This old school. This place where the Big Man ought to be.

"But some nut case up in Atlanta got hold this old schoolhouse a few months ago, Louie. He gonna turn it into offices, some art shops, maybe even a school again. Hell, that fruitcake even lives here when he ain't over screwing that gal on Houston Avenue. Now, with a gal like that, Louie, why would he want to hang around here? And why would he want to do anything with this old school house? I don't know, and I don't think you know. Anyway, we don't need this nut in Riverton. We still need this old town, and everything we are is in it. He don't need this school, either, and I suspect he will want to unload it before it's over. That's why we're here Louie. We need this school, and you're going to help me acquire this piece of property."

"Don't get you...."

One of them walked a few steps. Brooks shivered, and he tried to pick up the conversation again. He couldn't. The man's voice seemed strained; he talked in whispers, raised his voice suddenly, and whispered again.

"Yessir, we need the town and we need this place. That is, we can have it when we work it... if we don't get greedy... but in your case, mister math'matician, you done got greedy on me, Louie."

"Naw... naw now, that ain't so." Brooks clearly made out the protest. The other man continued in a mumble, but one with some distinct emotion to it now. Brooks thought the man must really hate Louie. There was a pause, almost as if the old man's thoughts were diverted by something. The old man stepped back down the hall, apparently into the teachers' lounge. In there, he said to himself: "This is where I learned the most... 'bout getting what I want."

"Boss, what you doing in there? There ain't nothing in there."

Another pause before the old man stepped out and erupted in rage.

"You skimming off me, Louie. And one thing this old school building didn't teach you was how to cheat me!" The mumbling groaned and the whispers spit out hisses. High-strung emotional hisses. "Fuck me in the ass... that old queer bastard... he didn't do it, now you won't neither!"

"Naw, don't, naw! Don't!"

Apparently Louie had stepped to the stairs, because when the shots rang out, five of them, Brooks could hear pounding on the steps, one at a time. Louie, it had to be Louie, must have stepped back to the stairs and down the stairs. He hit the stairs walking or rolling, Brooks couldn't tell, but the sound was feet dragging slowly across a sandy floor, a strange sound, followed by stumbling, bumping sounds and finally a thud, then something heavy sliding down the stairs. Brooks heard more bumps and bangs as Louie moved downward like a wayward tire rolling wildly or a steel drum bumping haphazardly over a rocky hillside. He heard Louie tumbling, though he couldn't see the splashes of blood left along the way.

The hall's draft brought the heavy smell of burnt gunpowder to the auditorium. Footsteps followed. The man wasn't hanging around to reminisce about the old days any longer. At first he hummed the tune to Riverton High's alma mater, the same one Brooks and students before and after him had sung a thousand times. But the old man got quiet as he started, slowly and cautiously, down the stairs at the south end of the hallway. The man exited the building from the basement door in the front -- the bottom floor, opposite from Brooks' apartment.

Brooks followed the footsteps with his ears. He heard the creaky back door slam shut and footsteps scuttle across the gravel. Across the playground, a vehicle's door open and closed, an engine started. Brooks looked out the window and watched as the vehicle's red rear lights disappeared into darkness down the street. The man, whomever he was, was gone. That was just before eleven o'clock. Brooks wasn't sure what to do, except that his teeth were chattering and he wanted to get warm. His trembling had progressed to near-convulsive shakes.

The brown sheriff's department cruiser rolled down North Houston Avenue through the darkness. The sheriff drove the car, and he hardly slowed in pulling into the county hospital's emergency entrance. He parked at the ambulance loading area, blocking two spaces and ignoring several signs warning, "No Public Parking!" He walked in through the back emergency room entrance to the hospital.

His unorthodox manner on investigations brought him to the hospital first, while most would have gone straight to the crime scene. Sheriff Carroll Johnson was an oddball, a loner, a book you couldn't read.

"Sheriff Johnson," Dr. Millgrove said.

The sheriff nodded and walked past as the doctor greeted before following the sheriff into a small office next to the emergency room. The sheriff entered first, with no deference to doctor and his office. While his boldness stopped short of sitting in the desk chair, the sheriff rested on a corner of the desk in a way that blocked the doctor from taking to his usual seat. The sheriff's face curled up into chubbiness around his mouth and eyes. It was a stone face, but one that could show expression.

"The body is in there, next to the operating room," the doctor said, showing slight exasperation and seeming to want the sheriff out of the office. "It's in pretty bad shape."

The sheriff didn't budge.

"Where's that boy from Atlanta? Told me he was here?"

"You mean Mr. Sheffield? He was here a moment ago."

"That's who I want to talk to. Say Ol' Louie lived awhile?"

"He was barely alive when they brought him in. Some signs, a heartbeat. Pronounced him dead a few minutes later."

The sheriff pondered that. Then he said: "Have 'em find that Atlanta boy, will you, Doc? Ol' Louie Basford can wait on us a little while."

"Nurse," the doctor called out the door. A young blonde woman came in, then left on the doctor's instructions to find Brooks Sheffield. As her crisp white skirt rounded the corner, a deputy, Charlie Wilkins, walked up to the office door. Wilkins, on night duty, called the sheriff about the shooting. He chewed his gum in staccato laps, loud and wet. And his eyes, topping off a long, clownish face, followed the young shapely nurse down the hall. He turned to the sheriff and doctor and blew a long, slow silent whistle.

"Who's out to the school, Charles?" the sheriff asked.

"We got Jamison up right after we called you. And Naughty and Sim is likely there by now. Sim, he just got off work at midnight... They's blood ever'where, Sheriff."

The sheriff seemed to ignore that last information.

"Better get on the horn and call the GBI. Tell Campbell to meet us at the old Graystone High School. Soon as I get through with this Sheffield fellow I'll get on out there. Tell you what, Charles, you stay right here at the hospital."

"Right."

Right, yes. The cute nurse was here, after all.

Brooks Sheffield walked into the office doorway and stood as Charlie, smacking away, eased on out looking down the hall again.

"Sheriff Johnson?" Brooks asked.

"You Sheffield?"

"Yessir."

"Come on in here and sit down. Thank you, Doc." The sheriff got up as the doctor left and shut the door.

"Have a seat, son," the Sheriff said, although Brooks was probably no more than three of four years younger than the official. "Now, what in hell went on out there tonight? And make it quick, we gotta go out there and meet the GBI."

Brooks told the sheriff how he came about living in the school. He said he heard noises outside around ten-fifteen or maybe a little later. He said he had been up in the school's attic. The sheriff asked Brooks why, on a chilly night like tonight, would he be up in the attic of an old school. Brooks said he was up there just sitting and looking out over the town, as he often did, particularly at night. The sheriff looked him straight in the eyes without saying anything else at that moment. Brooks went on to say he was coming out of the attic when he heard someone enter the building on the north side, he thought the back door.

"They break in or what?"

"I didn't hear glass breaking or the door being jimmied. I heard people walking up the north stairway. I went on up the second floor and hid in the auditorium. I couldn't see anything, but one of them grabbed a bucket for a seat. The one who was shot talked the most, but it was nervous talk."

"What you mean?"

"A lot of things. The man doing the shooting at first just sat there as if he was waiting for someone else. In fact, I heard this Louie guy ask him what was going on and who they were meeting."

"You recognize any of the voices?"

"The older man, and I think he was older, sounded familiar. But that could have been a long time ago. Nobody I've known since moving back. Louie referred to him as boss once."

"You hang out at the pool halls?"

"No. Louie did mention a pool hall, though."

"And what did he 'mention'?"

"Well, Louie apparently works in one. He referred to it in conversation. They were talking about what they had learned at the school. Louie talked about arithmetic..."

"Arithmetic?"

"Yeah. Right before Louie was shot, they talked about arithmetic. And some other things too, but I couldn't hear what the other man was saying. He whispered to Louie right before he shot him. He hissed at times, as if he were angry at Louie."

Uncharacteristically, the sheriff shook his head at this and smiled. He figured who the killer could be, but he felt it was a long shot and in no way did he let Brooks in on his speculation. So far, too circumstantial.

Then the sheriff got up and left the office as quickly as he had entered. In the hallway, he signaled the doctor down the hall, and then he walked directly into the emergency room. In a sterile, white side room, a body lay covered on a steel table. Tragedy poked through the sheet in blotches of brown-red, and spattered blood lay on the floor. Brooks followed the sheriff in, expecting this scene. Not waiting for the doctor, who was now entering the room, the sheriff lifted the sheet and stared down. He pulled the sheet back, down below the man's waist, and asked Brooks:

"This him?"

"Yep. I couldn't tell if he was alive when I first saw him and called the ambulance."

The sheet flew back down over the body, leaving an arm exposed.

"Come on, let's go over to your place."

"OK."

"You can ride with me."

Brooks followed, saying nothing else. They left the doctor and the young nurse to tidy the sheet over Louie. Charlie Wilkins watched.

Like his peers in other counties, Sheriff Johnson drove a big brown Ford Crown Victoria, in near perfect condition despite its being several years old and having right at 143,000 miles on the odometer. "Big county, heavy traffic," the sheriff said every time he went to the Piscola County commission for a new car. The county's traffic wasn't that heavy; he was referring to his driving a lot of miles and covering a wide territory in one of the state's largest counties. He had only a few deputies to help him, four to be precise, plus two full-time and one or two part-time radio operators, depending on whether Lucy Milteer was sober enough on any particular day to come in and help out. Mostly he drove alone, and he took on cases sometimes without involving anyone from his office.

They said little while riding over to the schoolhouse.

Twenty-three years with the Georgia Bureau of Investigation had taken a toll on W.D. "Dub" Campbell. His mission could have been an exciting one for any other law enforcement officer. He was one of only a few to cover several counties rife with drugs, first as a smuggling point for marijuana and cocaine and now for sales of crack cocaine and nearly anything else. This provided plenty for the GBI to do, especially in the attendant murders that came along with a robust drug trade.

Latinos and blacks outnumbered whites two to one or more in South Georgia. Only a few of the state's southern counties could be considered "economically viable," as the Georgia governor's economic task force studying the region had discovered. And those economies, though showing strength, remained small and tenuous.

Even so, South Georgia had made strides toward improvement. A banking company in a nearby town had bought and merged a lot of the area's smaller farm banks and was growing. A private health care center in in a bigger town was taking over the clinics and county hospitals. Thus sprang a health-care network bringing specialists once a week to the smaller towns. Cotton was coming back, and financing was under way for a big gin in Riverton. The peach and sweet corn crops were still good, and sunflowers and wheat were seen in some fields beside rows of tobacco and other crops.

For Dub Campbell, however, hope was lost. He was just short of fifty years old, stuck in a backwoods town smaller than where he started. Divorced. A daughter in Chicago who rarely called. Only one woman had interested him in recent years, and she was gone now. Others wouldn't put up for long with his job's dangers, its capricious nature and unpredictable hours. Murder, assaults, drugs and running moonshine and non-tax whiskey were the crimes, but the challenge of solving these, making arrests and sending criminals off for short prison stays -- or off scot-free -- was lost on Dub Campbell. The thrill of his job diminished long ago. It was a mere duty now, a task necessary to perform for a paycheck and, eventually, a state pension.

What was worse about Dub Campbell was his loss of vitality and the decline in his humor. As a football player at the University of Georgia, he had developed into an energetic and personable young man. His senior year caught him up in a romance with a Georgia cheerleader, and they married right after graduation. He started off with promise that in the last few years had deteriorated into hopelessness. His marriage finally broke up, splitting him not only from his life's love but damaging -- seemingly without chance of repair -- his relationship with his only child, a beautiful daughter named Julie. Dub Campbell was ready to feel good again, but he had no idea if he ever would. He had denied many of his problems for so long. Now, it was so obvious to him. He couldn't turn away much longer.

Dub Campbell had been a wake for more than an hour when the phone rang. Booze both put him to sleep and then kept him from sleeping. He was breathing heavily and smelling of bourbon fumes thick as gasoline when the phone rang. He moved his head and the brain buzzer went off, a steady, high-pitched hum.

"Hello."

"Yeah, Dub. This here's Charlie Wilkins, over at the hospital. We got a shooting. Dead right after we got him down here. Shot up at the old schoolhouse. Sheriff wants you when you get over there."

"Where? What school?"

"The old gray building on Webster Street. The one they don't use no more. You know the one."

"Oh. Be there."

Dub threw the receiver down and steadied himself on the bed. He didn't want to do this. He would. No time for a shower. He took one anyway. Cold.

He put on yesterday's slightly soiled and very wrinkled khakis, a clean white long-sleeved shirt and a wool sports jacket. No tie for Dub. He walked out to his car, a big state-issue, got in, and raced the engine. He pulled out and headed for Graystone High School.

His breathing picked up again and he knew his blood pressure was high. Get it checked, stop drinking, and eat right. That's what his doctor had told him years ago. He would do that. One day.

The big schoolhouse was creepy. Years before, Dub Campbell thought back, he could remember a similar feeling, couldn't put his finger right on it, but he was certain the past played a part in his reaction to this place. The halls smelled the same, save the dust. He could smell the paint, a gleaming government gray on all the walls in the basement and a slightly darker shade than the paint covering the building's exterior. This place couldn't have been painted any time recently, although he had heard some nameless person from Atlanta was fixing the school up. Yes, it smelled as fresh as September, when school opened and sweet-looking, shiny-nosed girls in new dresses and boys in blue jeans came back for another year of English, mathematics, science, home economics, the sawdust of shop, boxes of brittle new chalk, the grime of the gym and football field, and the flirtatious, playful and sometimes cruel chemistry of teenagers.

Dub walked down the hall toward a lighted room at the south end. He had entered the back doors at the building's north side. The sheriff's cruisers had been parked there, underneath an oak tree years older than the building. As he neared the doorway to the lunchroom, he looked down the hall leading to a stairwell. Then the memory hit him. There, underneath those stairs, he had kissed a girl the first time. Just finished the eighth grade and was spending the summer in Riverton with his grandparents. She was a trailer park girl, already in the tenth. It was 1954.

"Come on, Dubya Dee. There ain't nobody going to see us down here."

"I don't know Patsy, it's summer and the school's s'posed to be locked up."

"You chicken. Come on."

She took his hand and led him into the darkness of the hallway, down the corridor, lit dimly by the dusk light shining through the lunchroom windows. Dub followed reluctantly.

"Shhh." She stopped halfway down the hall.

"What?" he whispered.

She cocked her head, but kept walking.

"Nothing," she said, leading him to the south stairwell.

"Where we going, Patsy?"

She turned and he thought he saw her smile.

"Right here. Dub."

She reached up and kissed him. That was it.

"Pretty Dub. Bet all the eighth grade girls love you to death."

He fumbled with words.

"Come over here," Patsy beckoned with a wiggle of a finger and stepping backward. She rested her back against the wall next to the angled underside of the staircase. Then she pulled him close.

"Ever made out with a girl?" she asked.

Again, he fumbled, getting out only: "Well, ah, yeah, but..."

"Haven't really. Have you, Dub?"

He barely could see Patsy in the dark, but he could feel her body and her breath. She kissed him again, running her tongue underneath his upper lip. He was scared, but he enjoyed this, too. He kissed her. And when he did, she put her arms around him and rubbed her body into his.

"Mmm. Boy, howdy, you're not a bad first-time kisser, Dub."

He took charge and kissed her again and again. She fell against him and rubbed her breasts naughtily into his chest, and well he could feel her through his thin T-shirt. With this, Dub felt a rush of excitement. He backed off slightly.

Patsy wasn't talking much. She continued kissing him and rubbing into him. Then she put her head on his shoulder and rocked back and forth, as if they were dancing.

"I was dancing... with my darling... the night they... were playing... the beau-tee-ful Tenn-uh-see Waltz... Mmm. Hold on to me, Dub."

He did, pitching his groin back slightly. This must be heaven, he thought to himself as they continued to sway, adjusting to the discomfort all this brought.

Heaven. And hell.

Footsteps pounded down the staircase.

"Oh, heck! Let's go!" Patsy screamed.

The footsteps stopped as they ran for the opening and the hallway.

"Who's there? Stop!" Mr. Willis, the school principal, shouted.

Dub and Patsy ran down the hallway, stumbled over each other going up the steps and stopping to quickly look back. No one yet. They ran around the school, passed the tennis courts and darted through shrubs bordering the Lafayette Street sidewalk. The bushes helped them disappear long enough to look back and survey the building. Mr. Willis was at the back door, looking in their direction. They slipped down Lafayette to the corner, crossed Webster Street, and darted through more bushes and into a yard, continuing across the property to the back of a house. There they stopped and caught their breath.

Remembering this made Dub Campbell smile for a moment. Patsy, the girl from the other side of the tracks, who lived in a shotgun house in the mill town. That romantic occasion had been shot. But later, he remembered spending some wonderful evenings with Patsy all through that summer.

"Glad you could make it, Dub." Sheriff Carroll Johnson interrupted Dub's memories from the far end of the hall.

"Sheriff," said Dub, as he walked on down to the room in whose doorway the sheriff stood.

In the room were deputies Naughty Smith, Ralph Jamison and Sim Johnson, no relation to the sheriff. Dub nodded at the deputies and stood by the doorway. The room was strange. Years ago, it no doubt had been a small classroom, Dub thought. Some of the accouterments were still there: Wide windows, now covered in drapes, across the far wall; a black chalkboard on one wall scrubbed clean; another wall was a cork board, hardened with coats of paint.

Now the room was a kind of living quarters, simply furnished for a caretaker or someone more important, given the unusual touches of fine, old furniture -- and clothes a custodian would not wear. Against the outside wall was a double, four-poster bed and in one corner beside it was an open rack of a man's suits over which was a grate rack stacked neatly with starched and folded dress shirts. On one end of the long rack was a wooden coat hanger filled with an assortment of silk ties, all good quality. Deputies occupied two straight-back chairs. An empty brown leather Chesterfield armchair sat beneath a reading lamp in the corner to Dub's right.

The room had another door, in the corner opposite from where Dub was standing, with steps leading up to the outside. The steps had a heavy-gauge pipe railing passing from the upper outside door and down into the room. Beneath the railing and leading against the steps was a folding beach chair. In the inside corner, to Dub's left, stood an antique sideboard, on which were several bottles of bourbon, scotch and gin.

There was one other chair in the room, beside the bed. Naughty Smith, skinny as a bean pole, sat in it, his legs crossed, a cigarette smoldering between two long yellow fingers. A fuel oil heater, which reminded Dub of the type used in tobacco barns to cure leaves, crackled and occasionally bumped in the middle of the floor where the sheriff had stepped after beckoning Dub into the room.

Nobody said anything. They seemed to be waiting for someone else. Dub heard a toilet flush, then footsteps from up the hall. A man with brown but graying hair stepped into the doorway. His face was familiar, so familiar, although Dub could not place him right away. The man was from Riverton, and Dub was sure he had known him years ago, perhaps twenty-five or more.

The man looked up at Dub, extended a hand and said: "A ghost from your past. Brooks Sheffield."

Dub Campbell mustered something of his old self and

broke into a big, wide grin.

"Well, I'll be a sonofahogrootingbitch, Brooks!   Where you been, boy?"

Chapter 3 - Strolling

The schoolyard was finally quiet, resting after a late summer's day of children running through and scampering over broken-down bicycle racks and sagging tennis court nets. The man who lived in the gray school building walked outside to survey the evening calm in that season of solitude, months before Louie Basford's blood stained the school's north stairwell.

Occasionally in that solemn summer hour a car passed slowly, one in particular, the man noted, an early seventies Oldsmobile, a large car, with a muffler groaning and crackling. A man drove the car. The Schoolhouse Man thought that few white people came by this place anymore. He eased onto a lawn chair just outside the school's basement door, the door to his apartment, placing a copy of that week's Riverton Herald in his lap. He watched the man's car.

The Oldsmobile had stopped near the schoolyard's northwest corner. A young woman, just a teenager really, leaned into the driver's window. Soul music blasted from the car before a hand touched a knob, lowering the radio's volume. Conversation between the man and the teen picked up. The Schoolhouse Man bent his head, straining to hear. He heard nothing; what he saw was enough. The day's heat was easing off, and the Schoolhouse Man sat and listened to a conversation he could only see.

"Hey, baby."

"Yes, sir, Mr. T.J. How're you doing?"

"Not bad. You lookin' good, baby." T.J.'s eyes moved up and down as the teenager, looking not much older than sixteen, leaned farther into the car's window.

"When have we seen you?" the girl said.

"Too long, baby." He drew easily and long on a cigarette. "It's been too long." The man's leer seemed obvious to the Schoolhouse Man.

"Long enough, you comin' round here. My sister's done had her baby and you're comin' back round now are you, Mr. T.J.?" She chided him, but not too much.

"Mmm, honey." Their smiles were dazed and melting over each other's faces. "Let's go get some beer."

"Hey. Why would I want to do that?" she asked, teasing the man. The girl rested one foot on the other and rocked a knee back and forth. She leaned well into the car now, right in the driver's face, it seemed.

"Oh, you'll like what I got for you. Some real good stuff." The man grinned. He stroked the girl's arm with a finger. Then he opened the door and got out, standing by the car as the girl stood wide-legged by him. They talked a while longer, he repeatedly suggesting she ought to go with him and she putting him off with teases. Eventually, she climbed into the car.

"What's on your mind, T.J.?"

They drove away.

The Schoolhouse Man's eyes followed the car as it turned onto Webster Street and made its way slowly from the school. The engine droned away, fading into the night. The Schoolhouse Man stretched out in his lawn chair, sipped a bourbon and water. He could have been in his former suburban backyard in Atlanta.

He wasn't. He was in Riverton, Georgia, five hours by car south of the city and, in many ways, culturally and economically, years away from Atlanta. Yes, Atlanta now was so far away.

The night was clear, a good night for strolling down the town's sidewalks beneath shrouds of live oak and dangling Spanish moss. When the courthouse clock struck ten, the Schoolhouse Man pulled himself from the chair on that summer evening, folded it and placed it inside the former classroom he had converted to an apartment. He locked the door and walked toward Houston Avenue, imagining he had drifted back twenty years, then thirty years, then more, far more, to a time he neither knew nor remembered. It was a time that had eluded him forever. It was a time he came back seeking.

Brooks Sheffield, son of Riverton, Georgia, and owner of the town's stone-gray high school, contemplated the decrepit context of his times, an age of sadness and despair. Most people in his hometown owned nothing much anymore, some property, some cars, but that was all. People valued little, Brooks thought, other than cars and property. The thought of these things ordinarily would have made Brooks Sheffield dispense his will to live in such a place, where memories were his only balm to living and where old times -- the past of thirty years ago -- defined all his happiness. But this time and place were not so bad, and he found living under delusions of the past quite tolerable, more so than most people he knew. This place, to him, was an improvement over Atlanta.

Now, in Riverton, Brooks blended well with the confusion of the times. No one really questioned his living in the old schoolhouse building, although years ago friends and relatives might have tried to have him committed for doing such a thing. Today, in the Riverton of today, his behavior and lifestyle were nothing unusual, although attention-getting as they had been in the beginning. He now fell within what could be expected. To the town, Brooks Sheffield -- now that his grand plans for the school had slowed and thus quelled residents' imaginings of what he might do -- was no one in particular; to the children in the neighborhood, he was simply the Schoolhouse Man.

He walked the street with double lanes separated by parks. Oaks arched over both lanes of the street, and the night's darkness, captured and held by the great trees, fell all around him. Few people were out just after ten. Most houses were dark, save an occasional bedroom or porch lamp still shining through the oak leaves and moss.

Things might have changed in Riverton, but North Houston Avenue stayed much the same. It was the avenue of the people possessing what little wealth remained in the town. Some were different, he knew, newcomers. Professors from a college in nearby Valdosta had moved to Riverton for the turn-of-the-century houses in which they could live their own delusory existences. The grand houses still stood, with the exception of several gone to disrepair. One or two more recent structures had been built on the ashes of houses destroyed by flame or rot. When he passed the Methodist parsonage, itself a relatively new structure, he paused to look, then he walked down an alley connecting Houston with an access street that ran along the back entrances to the large houses. At the end of the alley, lights glowed from the other side of tall hedges. A game of tennis was in progress with the players saying little while scrambling to return a ball. Probably two college professors wrenching out the stress of combative academic politics, he thought. The Schoolhouse Man bent over to look through the hedge and see who was playing. No one he knew. He walked back to Houston.

Brooks turned back toward the courthouse square at the end of Houston. Two blocks from the square, Brooks saw Sara Compton sticking her head out a second floor window of her house.

"Brooks Sheffield," was her greeting as he walked past. "That you?"

"Yes. Evening, Sara."

"You enjoying the weather?"

"I'm trying."

"Come on up to the porch and sit."

Brooks stepped up the walk to the house and waited for Sara on the porch. Sara Compton and Brooks had known each other since grammar school. And in those thirty-five or so years, during most of which both lived elsewhere, a renewed friendship had only recently begun to blossom. All of a sudden, theirs was a common ground, one which for so long had seemed to ignore their presence but had finally brought them together.

In a small town, you know many people well and many others you may be acquainted with for a lifetime without ever really knowing them at all. Paths cross daily without people meeting or talking beyond necessary business. And people become no closer, other than knowing someone's name and what street they live on and where they go to church. Then, as life went on, people began to move away or die, and someone you always wanted to get to know no longer lived. Brooks found this to be true all too often. Some people weren't worth knowing, he thought, but Sara certainly was one.

They had little in common until now, and everything in their lives suddenly paralleled, although at the time he didn't know how much. To others, to anyone who didn't know the two and cared to think about the situation, they were quite different: Brooks living a near-eccentric life in the basement of the old high school, and Sara "retiring" from city life in Birmingham to come back to Riverton and finish her Ph.D. in English literature. She was a woman whose plain talk and easy manner attracted Brooks. They had seen each other several weeks ago as Brooks walked along Houston Avenue one evening. As he approached her house, he saw Sara watering the flowers by her front porch. Before he could say anything to her, she stepped over to the sidewalk, holding the hose back on the flowers, smiled broadly and introduced herself.

"You're Brooks Sheffield, aren't you?"

Brooks, caught not totally off guard, replied, "I am, yes. And I believe I know you, too."

"Sara Samples. You remember me, though, as Sara Compton, the name I've claimed again."

"Yeah, I thought that was you. You were something quite good on the basketball court, I remember."

"The team was. Those years were great fun."

Sara was modest. She was an all-state girls player for

three years, made high scorer in two state tournaments and played for state championship teams most years of high school. She had gone to the Auburn University and majored, as she told Brooks later, in finding marital bliss. She did marry after college, although happiness didn't follow. She and her husband had moved to Birmingham, where his job was, and she taught school; they'd had one son and eventually divorced. At forty-one she moved back to her late parents' home in Riverton. Her son, Robby, apparently was still in Alabama. But she didn't talk much about him, and Brooks didn't ask. Sara's mood changed when she had mentioned her son. It was the right time for her, she had said, returning to Riverton and working on her doctorate at Florida State University in Tallahassee.

"I thought about selling the house after mamma died," she had told Brooks that first night back in July. "But I really couldn't part with it. So one day I up and moved back to Riverton. It was an easy decision, really, especially with FSU's program so close by. We make life so complicated, then all the decisions, the great life decisions come so easily sometimes, usually by the help of circumstances. I left everything in Birmingham and moved back here where I had nothing but a house, the furniture in it, my studies and some family friends. Moving back here was an easy decision in some ways..." Sarah's mood dimmed, and she just stared at the spray of water on the flowers.

Brooks remembered what he said that night, his contribution to Sara's assessment of her decision. He said: "Circumstances do move you. It helps if you live in an old schoolhouse. There, few of life's normal complications intrude."

She had smiled again. "And that's where you live?" she had asked, intrigued by the notion and stifling a giggle as she jerked the water hose down onto the grass, then bringing it back on the flowers. "I had heard talk around town about the Schoolhouse Man."

Brooks paused, staring off at a street lamp and the bugs

darting in and out across the bright light. Then he said, "Yes, I do. I live over on Webster Street in the old schoolhouse. Down in the basement. Near the science lab. I am, I guess, the Schoolhouse Man."

"Well, I have heard everything now," Sara said. "How did you manage that?"

"Simple. One of those easy decisions. My father left it to me."

Sara laughed at that. In laughing, she touched Brooks' arm, one folded over the other in his shirtsleeves. She touched his arm in the way Southern women do so gently and lovingly. She left her hand there a moment, squeezing his arm before letting go.

"You really got people's attention when you first moved in. Weren't you going to renovate it for offices or something?"

"Yeah, I had some great plans. Still do."

"That is just absolutely Brooks Sheffield. Living in a schoolhouse," she said. "You were the dramatic type in high school, and I always thought you were a little strange."

Sara laughed again, and Brooks smiled. Then they went up and sat on the porch. That was a month ago. And since then they had been sitting and talking one or two and, lately, three or more nights a week.

On this night, Brooks headed for the porch and sat down to wait for Sara. When she emerged, she was dressed in a nightgown and a light cotton robe. The robe was buttoned midway and the top was parted, showing the lacework on the gown, the fine stitching of lilacs dancing amid delicate green leaves and vines. Brooks glanced down one side of the gown's V-neck and then up the other.

"Make yourself at home," Sara said, sitting down in the big cushioned rocker. "I'm relieved August is so wet, given the cooler temperatures the rain brings," she told him.

Brooks rocked, surprised in a way at the comment. He thought they had gotten well beyond talking about the weather.

"It's wet and not too hot," she went on. "Not bad for a South Georgia summer."

"Not bad, t'all," was Brooks' comment. He was at ease, having drunk two bourbon-and-waters at the schoolhouse. Sara rocked back as if reclining and held the position with her toes against the porch rail before easing back down. Then they both rocked gently as they looked out on the street.

Brooks reflected on the moment. Thirty years ago, sitting with a woman, or a girl, like Sara, would have been difficult for him. When he was sixteen, knowing girls had been arduous until he met Jane and fell in love. He had shied from most girls, and even in later years he found comfort with only certain women; his type fell in a "narrow threshold," as a woman colleague had called them, and few fit it. Since moving back to Riverton and into the old school, he saw few women socially and all those were convenience dates to cocktail parties at the college in Valdosta or to an event at the country club. On most of these occasions, the relationships were little more than two people sharing a ride.

Now he felt at ease with Sara, who struck him as enjoyable and wholly a beautiful woman. Her skin was smooth and lightly tanned; her breasts, round under the gown and robe, looked as firm as the sixteen-year-old ball player she once had been; her hands were strong and veiny. Her face was pretty and offered an excited, bright-eyed openness. Sara, he remembered, could be stern and command attention, as had many of those girls on the basketball court. Few were shy, most were smart, and they all carried the confidence that came with victory and success. But if winning imparted self-assurance and certain haughtiness, Sara showed none of that now.

Sara suggested having a drink, and Brooks accepted. She went into the house and in a few minutes came back with a tray of glasses, ice, bottles white wine and seltzer. As she set the tray down, she said, "I suppose it's getting late for a drink."

"Yes," Brooks replied. He helped prepare the drinks,

pouring the wine and topping each glass off with seltzer.

"Oh, heavens, make it light, please," Sara said, taking the drink and sitting down. Brooks poured her water and handed over a spoon, then fixed his drink. Sara sat back in the rocker.

"This is to future friendships and to all those years we did whatever we were doing. May those years rest in peace," Sara said, smiling and holding up her glass. Their glasses clinked, and they both sipped the wine cooler.

"Time is never kind to us when we're young," Brooks said, his mood cheerfully philosophical. "It creeps along, then catches us, and fools us. And we don't know what time has done until we're old and it's too late to change a thing."

"That's true," said Sara.

She stared out at no place in particular on the street. Then she turned to Brooks and smiled. Back to the street, she surveyed again that ground of retreat their eyes found when nothing was being said, or when what they said ventured too close to what should remain unstated. They had shared each other's company for weeks now but no intimate words had broached any direct expression or a hint, for that matter, that one or the other cared to pursue a relationship beyond summer evenings on the front porch.

"At least, it's true enough for you drama types," she added. "And you're as philosophical as you are dramatic."

Sara laughed and so did Brooks.

"I guess my lingering eventide mood in me is coming forth," he said. "About time and the world. What I don't know is why we cage ourselves the way we do and the way we cage others, and others us."

"You mean the rat race, or what?"

"Yes, the rat race, some used to call it. The chaotic contest for survival. Don't know why we do it. It's a constant, though. Most people do it until they die," Brooks said, his gaze toward the street.

"Except thee and me, to some extent," Sara said. "I guess people must laugh at you now, and me, for doing what we're doing, I mean, dropping out? Being hippies? You know, twenty years ago, we would be hippies, living off little and using our family property to survive. And me, over-educating myself. The ultimate escape is forever in school."

"Yeah, and ten years ago, yes, they would laugh and talk. And some people, I'm sure, are now," he said. "But most don't, not today in Riverton. Things have changed some, but not all that much. Twenty to thirty years ago appearances definitely made you or killed you in this town."

"I remember."

"One thing I've noticed in the few weeks I've been back is this: All the white folks basically live on one street, this one right out here. A few live elsewhere, but most of them live right out here. A college professor at the school in Valdosta lives over there. You know her. She's like you, divorced and lives alone. A man who's a banker in Valdosta and his wife live down where the Bullocks used to live, that big house by the funeral home. The Riverton Farmers Bank president lives in the next block. And the guy whose daddy bought the paper from me lives several blocks up that way. The rest do various things, most outside this town. But they are all white. Hell, and this town's mostly black now. All we have is a black school superintendent and a black police chief. Many of the rest are poor and out of work. We've got to change that."

"Well, not all the white folks work, either, me and you included. At least, until I get my degree and a job at the college in Valdosta, I hope. Still, I'm living off family and the slim proceeds of divorce."

"Yeah. Us white folks have our own kind of welfare. Our families' money or property or business or what money we could get from selling any of that, in my case. I guess they thought I was crazier than hell for selling Daddy's newspaper, then moving back here and living in the old school. But then, I helped their notions along from an early age."

"You did, you did," Sara giggled, managing to shift the

conversation. "I remember your craziness nearly set the schoolhouse on fire once."

"The rocket? Yeah, we had been to Tennessee that summer and we loaded up on fireworks. The good kind. Not those silly little firecrackers they sold down here. I remember we made a rocket out of a dozen or more skyrockets."

"You all called it the Spaceship Riverton," I remember.

"Yep, and Mr. Simpkins in twelfth grade physics thought he had inspired some space scientists, for certain, although our endeavors were not of a scientific nature. When we launched that sucker 'side the school, everybody looked straight up. But the rocket made a beeline side trip from the launching pad and shot through Mrs. Sikes's English class window on the second floor. Glass went everywhere. I guess Dante was exciting as hell that day."

"My sister was in that class," Sara said. "She said the whole class thought they dropped right into the Inferno, all that hellfire and damnation erupting when the rocket landed in flames. Mrs. Sikes nearly died. Jimmy Felton started praying out loud. She said most all the girls were screaming and carrying on. And Janie Maxwell's period started. 'Course it made it sort of a better story that old Mrs. Sikes was reading from Dante out loud when it hit."

They laughed and drank.

"What are you going to do with that old schoolhouse?"

"I had big plans, but I was moving too fast so I've slowed things down," he replied. "One of the reasons I came down here was to slow down. Eventually I'd like to rent part of it back to the school board for offices or storage or even some classrooms, which are in pretty good shape on the first floor. I even have some bigger ideas. We have to do something about the poverty cycle of this town. I'm thinking of a job-training center there, if I can get someone interested. Anyway, I'll be painting and fixing everything for that this winter. No rush. Won't take much work, mainly cleaning and painting. The school was in good shape. They used it for various things until recently."

"So you may have some company over there one day?"

"Yep."

Sara was smiling, but the thought of intruders in his beloved schoolhouse made Brooks think again about his plans. Sara excused herself and went inside. A few minutes later, Brooks heard the music, only slightly at first but enough to tell Sara had put on a record. Then the volume grew. The tune drifted to him slowly, only familiar at first, then he remembered and began mouthing the words as Roy Orbison sang "Blue Angel." Orbison was singing "I'm Hurtin'" by the time Sara returned with more ice.

Brooks' mood lifted with the music and Sara's presence. The wine helped, too, and he was high enough to ask her, so he did.

"Want to dance?"

"Yes, sir. I do."

Brooks rose from the rocker and took Sara's waiting hand.

She closed her eyes, and the music took them across the porch and back, way back, to some other time. They listened and danced to "Running Scared," and on "Crying" Brooks held Sara real close. They each dreamed in the dancing, about a date, someone special if only for one short evening. Everyone all around them was dressed in formal attire, girls in strapless gowns with puffy ruffles, boys in white dinner jackets; a few boys had on suits. It was 1959, and the band played the fast-tempo rock'n'roll hits of the day along with an occasional ballad for slow dances. Brooks imagined smelling the corsage and the perfume, and he remembered that whatever the perfume was, it smelled like sweet hand soap. A strong user of sweet hand soap, his date. That or she wore some exotic perfume unfamiliar to the young Brooks Sheffield, freshman newspaper reporter, debate alternate and a shy young man with the girls, and certainly with this one. This was a sweet girl, too, tan like Sara in complexion, familiar with the social graces and very polite. The night, back then, was cool after the heat of a September football game day. Fall was nearing. Brooks was nervous. They danced every slow dance. That was it. And when his father picked them up at midnight, they both got in the Ford sedan's front seat and quietly rode home. No kiss at the door, just a polite thank you. She squeezed his hand and went inside. His first dance date had ended.

On the porch, Sara's large front porch, they rocked and swayed to the music. The feel of Sara close to him brought Brooks back. He looked down to Sara's face resting on his shoulder. She was shorter than he remembered from high school. She brought her head up and gazed into his eyes.

"What are you thinking?" she asked.

Brooks paused, finally replying, "Memories. They're wonderful, don't you think?"

Sara didn't answer with words. Her lips broke into that graceful, beautiful smile that Brooks fell over several weeks ago, and she rested her head on his shoulder again. They danced the same pace, an easy rocking, through all Orbison's songs. Brooks picked it up slightly on "Candy Man" and "Dream Baby," but he didn't care for the romp of these songs. He hated dancing. At least, until this moment.

They rocked slowly to a stop, although the music went on. For awhile they stood there holding onto one another. Sara hummed softly with the music as Orbison sang "Blue Bayou." They swayed gently. And on one part, Sara sang along with Roy: "I'm going back someday, come what may, to Blue Bayou... Where you sleep all day, and the catfish play... Mmm..."

"Blue Bayou," Brooks said after the song ended. "That's what I used to think of this town."

"What's that?"

"I used to think of this place as a kind of Nirvana. A Mecca. It's a place in your mind. You leave places like this thinking you never want to come back. And years later you think back, on childhood, on growing up and on none of the things that convinced you to get out. You fool yourself that those times and this place were everything wonderful and complete about life. You, rather I... hell, everybody... is fooled about memories and starlit nights and the touch of virginal breasts as you dance with a beautiful, blonde farm girl. We confuse memory with longing. Memory clouds it. And we make the fatal mistake of going back, or trying to. I did. Hell, I'm still trying to walk back to a better time. The good old days."

"They are here, right now, those good old days, Mr. Sheffield," Sara said, conjuring the admonition to a different generation of the early seventies -- so much different from their time and their town of the late 1950s.

Brooks looked into her eyes, leaned down and kissed her. For him, then, kissing Sara on her porch, there was no past and no need for one. And for a moment, Brooks Sheffield, king in his world of melancholy and loneliness, felt happy. They kissed long and held each other close.

"Yes, Miss Compton, these are the good old days. They sure are."

"Please, call me Sara."

"Yes, ma'am, Sara," he said.

They kissed again, before going inside.

Chapter 4 - Gini

Sam Warren kept everything he needed to know in a small, wire-bound notebook in the chest pocket of his brown plaid suit jacket. This notebook contained the accounting figures for his pool halls and liquor stores. In the left front pocket of his pants, which never matched the jacket, he kept a money wad and a driver's license. That was all. His accounting next to his chest, his money near his other personal assets.

Sam Warren was as serious about maintaining a close watch on his business and valuables as he was on seeking entertainment, which in turn was just as simple and straightforward. He enjoyed only the company of a woman with curves and an occasional drink. He pursued sex often and took a drink usually as a prelude to intercourse or as a cool-down afterward.

At seventy-three, he had outlived many of his early lovers. And in some cases, he had outlived his first lovers, their husbands and even some of their children. Sam had never married. Why bother. He could have most women he wanted, and to anyone he couldn't have he paid little thought. He recognized many desirable women were out of bounds, although women with husbands had caught his attention, and affection, many times; others, without husbands, held their own kind of pitfalls. He stayed away from widows, as a rule; they usually wanted something permanent, something to replace what they had lost or what they never had, whichever the case. He also avoided younger women, other than prostitutes. As to whores, he always opened his home to those who worked for him, and he had been known to fetch two or three whores at a time from Orlando, Tallahassee or Jacksonville and put them up at his farmhouse for a week or so.

Sam truly played the field, whether he was paying directly, in the case of the women of the night, or paying indirectly, or "in kind," as he put it, by buying clothes or a trip to Atlanta or even a new car for some of his other girlfriends. As another rule, he never went with a woman longer than four to six months. And he never fell in love with someone he couldn't have for his immediate enjoyment.

The one exception -- perhaps the reason for the rule -- occurred in 1953. He fell in love with the preacher's wife. Virginia Gilchrist. Sam was younger then, and at the time he was feeling a need to settle down and maybe have a family. He went to church during this time but was frustrated by the rejection from the young women in the church. Even widow women and old maids desperately seeking a husband had shunned him. Then the church got a new preacher, the Rev. James C. Gilchrist. Mrs. Gilchrist, with blonde hair, dressed as fine as any Atlanta lady Sam had ever seen. A former beauty queen from Mississippi, she talked often and openly about almost anything, thus immediately establishing a "reputation" in the congregation of being brash. Many women avoided her, but nearly all remained nice enough to her face. This, of course, presented a problem for the Rev. Mr. Gilchrist. It gave Sam an opportunity. He saw Mrs. Gilchrist as a victim, much like himself. Both were outcasts from the closed, tight world of small-town Baptists. He first pursued her in conversation at church social events. Soon it moved beyond that, and he found himself seeking her out during the week, anytime her husband was visiting at the nursing home or out of town for a ministerial association or other meeting.

Gini Gilchrist seemed to enjoy meeting Sam. He would drop by the preacher's house with a sack full of peaches or beans or sweet corn. They would chat in the kitchen, Gini serving him coffee or iced tea. Sam remained cautious. He knew that visiting the preacher's wife at her home could not go unnoticed in this gossipy Baptist community for long, so he devised a way to draw the minister's wife to him, regularly.

At that time, in addition to pool halls, Sam owned several blocks of shotgun houses, which he rented to the working poor. His father owned this property before him, and at one time the houses had been part of a small mill town surrounding his grandfather's cotton gin. Sam was not nearly as ruthless with his renters as his father had been; he figured these people had no place else to live. So instead of just collecting rent, keeping them in entrenched poverty and losing a house here and there to vandalism, misuse or arson, he tried to give something back to the little community. He helped Ella Wilson establish a mission in the neighborhood and provided her space for church services in an empty corner store. He felt the church now needed a little something extra. And one day, to set his scheme for Gini Gilchrist in motion, he went to visit Ella Wilson.

He drove down to the church in his black, dusty Buick and found Ella in the back of the building unpacking a crate of used hymnals that had been donated by the Methodist church.

"Lord, Mr. Sam," Ella said when he walked in. "We don't sing half these hymns. But I reckon they're appreciated, just the same. Missus Carter just dropped them by. She's a good lady, that Mrs. Carter. How you doin', Mr. Sam?"

"Oh, Ella, I'm fine," he said to the point. "Fact, I got something I think you can help me with."

"Oh, what's that?" Ella sounded cautious. Sam Warren had been good to her, but she was forever wondering when he might come down, close down the church and open up a beer hall in the neighborhood.

"Well, Ella, you know there's a new preacher up there at the Baptist church."

"Ahn, huh."

"He's got this pretty little wife and she, well, she don't have a thing to do in town. She sits up in that pastorium all day long. Tell you the truth, Ella, not many of the Baptist ladies are really having anything to do with her, she's so pretty. Anyway, Ella, she's looking to help people. She wants to. And I was thinking, what with the kids you have over here after school, maybe she could help you out. You know, games, cookies, and Bible stories. Things like that."

"Well, yeah, Mr. Sam. You know, we always need help here. People in this neighborhood don't help much, a few of the mamas do sometimes, but mostly they don't. They just send their kids over."

"'Course, Ella, I don't want to appear meddling. But you'd have to ask her. You know, I don't hang around the Baptist too much and it ain't like I could walk right up and get you two together."

Ella grinned, knowing Sam Warren was lying. He had been going to church up there at Trinity Baptist for more than a year and how else would he know about the Mrs. Gilchrist's free time. Everybody in town knew it and talked about how the owner of the pool hall might be, just might be, getting religion. She always knew he had a heart. But he wasn't a man for the church, she knew that, too.

"I'll ask her. I sure will, Mr. Sam. I'll be up at the church tomorrow morning to pick up some canned goods. I'll drop by the house and ask her. Yes, I will."

"Well, good, Ella. I think it'll be good for both of you." With that he left, satisfied he had accomplished what he wanted.

In no time, Gini Gilchrist was visiting the little black mission church several times a week to help Ella. Sam drove up one Thursday afternoon to initiate his regular visits.

"Why, look who's just walked in the door, the devil himself," Gini proclaimed.

Ella looked up, not at all shocked by the incongruity of this woman. This white woman, this preacher's wife spoke out more than anyone Ella had ever known. No wonder the Baptist women of Riverton shunned her. For Ella, she liked Mrs. Gilchrist and saw her as a great help in the mission work. She told Gini Gilchrist of Mr. Sam's benevolence, but she never mentioned his suggestion to involve the preacher's wife in the mission work.

Sam strolled in, smiling and nodding his head. "My Lord, I don't know who's working who the most. Ella you, or you Ella," he said.

"Well, I'll tell you one thing, Sam Warren," Gini replied. "You come sashaying in here talking like that and you'll be the one scrubbing and dusting and fixing oatmeal cookies!"

They all laughed, and Sam teasingly made an abrupt about-face and started for the door. He stopped in the doorway and turned back around. Four children ran in from the back door, picked up toys and starting playing.

"Here they come now," Gini said. "Children, remember that story we read Tuesday about George Washington. Well, this is his brother, Uncle Sam."

"He really?" said one of the children.

"He sure is. That's Uncle Sam of the United States of America. George Washington's brother. Yes sir!"

Sam grinned and turned red as the children clambered around him. Ella and Gini laughed as Sam was momentarily trapped by the children's attention.

He let them hold his hands and swing around. He forced a smile and looked into Gini's happy eyes. Sam Warren was in love.

He let a week go by, and timed his second visit for later in the afternoon. He rolled up at just before six o'clock. Gini was still there, but Ella had left to walk several of the younger children home. He went in the back door and found Gini kneeling on the floor, picking up pieces of several jigsaw puzzles scattered in a corner.

"Howdy do."

Gini jumped and nearly fell over, catching herself with a free hand and dropping the collected puzzle pieces.

"My gracious, Sam! You scared me nearly to death."

"I'm sorry." Sam was standing over her, offering a hand. She accepted and stood up.

"Haven't seen you around the last week or so."

"I guess I've been a little shy. 'Fraid you all might put this old boy to work. Real work."

There were those smiling eyes again. Recovering from the start, she was breathing hard. Her breasts, covered by a slip and thin blouse, moved up and down. A silk scarf was tied around her neck.

"We'll do just that, I assure you."

He stooped to pick up the puzzle pieces.

"Oh, Sam, really. I can do that."

"Nope. I scared you to death, so I can at least do this. Besides, you look like you need to get out of here and get home. Getting late. You shouldn't be down here after dark. Preacher will need his supper."

"Well, it's early. And Jim's going to be late."

"Still, you shouldn't stay down here by yourself."

"Well, with a big strong landlord like you around here, I feel pretty safe."

Sam smiled at that, his point fading with her words. He wanted to touch her right then, to hold her and kiss her. He resisted. She seemed like a forward woman, and had she not been a preacher's wife he already would have taken her in a long embrace.

She turned and walked to the back room.

"Ella will be back soon. I thought I would clean up and wait for her."

"Fine. I'll help you if you promise not to work me too hard."

"Nothing left to do, really. A few plates to take home. That's all."

He followed her to the back room. Her hips swayed smoothly with the movement of her legs, which were young and muscular. Her calves were full and flowed down into a thin ankles and narrow feet, fitted in brown heels. Her skirt was brown, lighter than the shoes, and too tight for a preacher's wife, he thought. Her blonde hair, today pulled up loosely off her neck in perfumed silk, bounced lightly with her walk. The blouse, the thin blouse, buttoned in the back.

And through the thin material he saw a wide bra strap with multiple fasteners. In many ways, Gini Gilchrist was like a woman Sam had dated in Jacksonville several years previous. That woman -- outspoken and big boned, much larger than Betty, and big breasted -- had filled his life so wonderfully. He wanted Gini Gilchrist. He desired her. He loved her.

Sam had not attended services at the church for several Sundays. He had found what he wanted, after all, his church life having served its purpose. His desire for the preacher's wife, however, meant frustration, and it presented an uncomfortable situation. He had no need to cause trouble with a married woman. He never had done that. If married women had been his before, he had never forced his way with them. Always, the affair had been mutually sought and short. Never had it aroused the suspicion, to his knowledge, or ire of a husband, primarily because Sam never slept with a married woman living in Riverton. His hometown was special to him. He liked calm waters, and he kept touchy situations away, removed from Riverton.

So when he walked into the church service that Sunday morning he was surprised to see a visiting preacher in the pulpit chair usually occupied by the Rev. Mr. Gilchrist, who was conducting a revival the next two Sundays in Americus. Sam sat through the service thinking of missed opportunities with Gini. Maybe he should be bold enough to drive up to Americus that week and "happen" to meet her. That was too much. He had to get his mind off her. He could leave town a few days, but he didn't need to follow her to Americus.

As these thoughts went through his mind, his eyes moved around the sanctuary. Baptist hats and Baptist suits and Baptist smells packed the church. As he scanned the browns, muted greens and dark blues, he spotted a red hat on the opposite side of the sanctuary. A red hat with a long pheasant feather stuck in it. He could almost detect the feather's marbling greens, speckled browns and reddish tint, and he could see underneath the hat a turn of blonde hair. Gini?

The congregation stood up for the benediction, and Sam leaned over to try to see under the red hat. No clue. Couldn't be her. He had never seen Gini Gilchrist dressed in bright red, a color nearly too bold even for a Mississippi beauty queen. There was a long benediction, then began the social exchange as the congregation filed out and everyone greeted everyone else, shaking hands, smiling, nodding, talking tales of football and who beat whom the afternoon before and who died the week before and who was sick this Sunday.

Sam's head moved around the crowd. Several people spoke to him, one going so far as to say they had missed him in Sunday school.

Damnwellbetcha, Sam thought, I missed you folks, too.

The crowd milled toward both the back and front doors, some going one way, others moving in the opposite direction. He lost the red hat, but picked it up again at the front of the sanctuary. Its owner was bent over slightly, shaking hands and talking with a little old woman who must have been ninety. Someone else walked up behind the red dress and the hat turned.

Gini! Her lipstick matched the dress and hat. She looked divine. Sam's heart raced. He wanted her. Relief released some of the torment inside Sam, and now, he knew, she had stayed home while husband preached a week in Americus, home of peanuts and the top-ranked high school football team in the state that season.

He went out the front door and down the street to his car and drove out to his farm. Tomorrow he would pay a visit to Ella Wilson's mission church, and he would have a little Halloween surprise for all the children. And one for Gini Gilchrist.

On Monday afternoon Sam sent W.H. Simpkins, who ran Riverton's Corner Pocket Pool and Recreation Parlor, out to the A&P for some Halloween candy. He told W.H. to buy a lot, that he was giving the regulars some to take home to their kids. W.H., who didn't know what to think of all this, obliged his boss with four big grocery bags full of Reese's cups, his own personal favorite, along with a dated receipt.

Sam made an entry in his notebook, then wadded up the receipt and threw it away. He told W.H. to give three bags of the candy away to the regulars. Then he took the fourth and went out to his car. He drove over to the Gilchrist home, parked down the street and took out a fountain pen. On the back he wrote, "Happy Halloween to all the mission children. Uncle Sam." Then he walked up to the pastorium, tucked the bag inside the screen door, rang the bell several times quickly and ran back to his car. In a few minutes, the door opened, and Gini picked up the bag. She read the note, looked around, and went back inside. Sam drove off. At six o'clock he arrived at the mission. Gini was they're cleaning up, alone.

"Ho. Ho. Ho. Merry Halloween," Sam said.

"Since when did Santa Claus come on Halloween?" she said.

"Since he was me."

"The kids enjoyed the candy. You were thoughtful to think of them. Between what was in that bag and my pumpkin pie, they won't have to eat for a week."

"Where's Ella?"

"She's not feeling well today. I sent her home with a bunch of the little kids and told her I would lock up and not to worry about coming back."

"Well, good. Perhaps I can help."

"You've done enough. Besides, you don't work well. I suspect it's because you do so little work, Uncle Sam." She was smiling. Sam was used to her constant joking.

"Yeah. That's me. Mister leisure life."

They were both standing at a little table in the back room. Gini began packing up paper witches and jack-o'-lanterns and skeletons and collecting paper plates and napkins for the trash.

"Gini," Sam said. His serious tone caught her attention immediately. She looked up at him. "Gini, you know, I told Ella to ask you to do all this."

"Is that right?"

"Yes. I figured she probably told you, but..."

"Told me?"

"Well, I needed to see you... often, and this was one way to do it..."

"Well, Sam, that's fine. But I'm doing this for Ella and the children. If you want to see me as a friend, you know, join my Sunday school class or see me at church. I'm there a lot during the week and Sundays."

"No, Gini. That's not what I mean."

"What do you mean, exactly, Sam?" She met his gaze, glanced down quickly and then resumed packing decorations into a cardboard box.

That breathing again! He could see that her breasts, today partially obscured underneath a sweater, were moving up and down. She was excited, probably alarmed by his presumptuous approach.

"You..." Sam hesitated. He usually was sure of himself but this was a serious step. He looked at Gini, reasoning they were both grown people. He moved closer to her. Then he said: "Ours is far more than friendship, Gini. I'm mad about you." He touched her shoulder. She stood there, not backing off, and his confidence grew. He had thought it out, though, and resisted embracing her.

"Sam," She looked down a moment before bringing her beautiful eyes back to his. "I think a lot of you, too. But, I..."

"Don't say anything, Gini." He reached up and pulled the switch on the light dangling above their heads. "No need for anybody seeing us talking in here like this. I have to tell you something..."

"But Sam..."

"I've only been going to church for a short time. A year, maybe a little longer. I'll tell you why I started going to church. It had nothing to do with religion. I came looking for a wife."

"Well, Sam I think that's the place to find a good wife -- the church."

"Maybe for most men. Not for me. My name, my family's name, doesn't mean much here. 'Specially with the Baptists, even though my grandmother was the rock of this church. As long as she was living, I went every Sunday. But my folks were different. My mother was an Episcopalian. She went to services in that church, but left me alone with my father when it came to religion. My father, of course, was like my grandfather. Neither one of them set foot in the church in my memory. And my father, he owned the pool hall here all his life. The Baptists don't take to drinkin'. You know that. At least they profess not to. Now I'm in the pool hall business, too, and I own a liquor store in Valdosta. They don't think much of that. So I'm an outcast. And I hate to be critical, but I'm a little like you in that. I guess they accept me to some degree because of my grandmother and because when I was young I went to that church. Until my grandmother died, anyway."

She stood there looking at him, not saying anything.

"So the women at the church stay clear of me," he went on, "thinking, I guess, that I'd be the last person they would marry. Surely, you know what I mean?"

"Yes. Sam," she said, putting a hand on his arm and sitting back on the table. "A preacher's wife is either loved or hated. Usually she's loved if she's pretty and keeps her mouth shut because everybody wants to be like her. They adore her. But if she gets out of line, says the wrong thing at the wrong time, then she's labeled a trouble maker, not worthy, sassy, above everybody else. Is that what you mean?"

"Yeah."

"Well, if that's what you mean then, yes, I know how you feel."

Sam put his hand around her waist, leaned over and kissed her gently on the lips. She didn't resist the kiss, but she also had second thoughts.

"Sam, I... that's what I mean, Sam," she said. "I can't do this. You obviously have feelings for me that I can't return. You have to forget all this." She pushed him away, and brought her knee up on the table for a measure of distance between her and him. He moved forward and brushed her knee with the front of his pants. With this, she moved off the table and walked around it.

"Sam," she said, looking down at the carved pumpkin jack-o'-lantern on the table. "Sam, I have to go now."

"Why, Gini. I don't mean to pry, but I know you spend a lot of time alone up there in that house that sits across from the church. You don't seem to get much attention. From him or any man. I care about you. You can't be happy with a preacher. With him, anyway."

"Sam, how can you say that?"

He moved around the table. She didn't step back.

"Gini, that's really not the point. And I'm sorry I said that. But still I think it's true. You're a woman who's full of life and you deserve to have everything."

He put a hand on her neck and drew her lips to his. He kissed her hard. Her hand pushed against the breast pocket of his jacket, feeling the wire-bound notebook inside, the notebook that recorded the transactions of his businesses, the pool halls and the liquor store. She pushed more, but she didn't fight him hard enough. They kissed long, and he held her neck firmly in one hand. She pushed back again and when he leaned into her face, she turned, grimaced, bringing her head tight into his chest.

"No, Sam. Oh... Sam." She tried to push him away, but he held on to her and felt her breasts against him. She breathed heavily, up and down. The air entered her lungs and blew into his mouth. He kissed her neck and felt her breath on his ear. She succumbed at last, placing her hands around his neck and running fingers over the stubble of a fresh haircut.

He slid the sweater off her shoulders and moved both hands to the back of her blouse and to its buttons. Gingerly he unbuttoned each one as he kissed her neck and her hands massaged the back of his head before clasping his shoulders. He pulled the blouse off and meticulously unfastened her bra.

He dropped both garments on the table, stood back and looked at her. She crossed her arms over herself and stood up, away from the table, shaking her head. He looked at her breasts. He moved powerful hands under her and lifted her back on the table. It wobbled under her weight, and the jack-o'-lantern slid and crashed to the floor, its toothsome grin split as the shell smashed into shards of pumpkin shell. He embraced her again, moving both hands along her legs. Her hands pushed, but she didn't fight him off.

He's so powerful, Gini thought as she began to cry. Her muscles stiffened, but her resistance gave way to weakness against Sam's strength. She fell into a dreamlike state, feeling so much about the moment and understanding only that things were moving so quickly, beyond all her control.

By the time she managed to say, "Oh, Sam... No," he had already entered her. The table wobbled and rocked to their rhythm. He finished too soon and felt tears and saliva pooled at the bottom of his neck.

"My Dear Sam,

"You know I cannot see you again. We're moving, for one thing, mainly because people never cared to have me around here. So Jim's getting another church. I just wanted you to know our leaving wasn't because of you. But we couldn't go on. I love Jim and I can't forsake him. I have to go with him. I won't say I don't love you. Please don't try to see me and don't ask me if I do. What we did was terrible. It cannot happen again. I take the blame. I'm too outgoing for my own good. You didn't know that I just like you the way I like most people. I just can't let that happen again. So long, and may we keep one love in common, the love of Jesus, our Savior.

"Sincerely, G."

Sam Warren thought about that letter a lot. He didn't keep it. The letter, as paper, was an unimportant pink, flimsy thing. What it contained let him down for the rest of his life.

Love unsecured and unreturned, a love so shortly lived. The day he received the letter he read it several times, then destroyed it. But he carried the words around a long time. He never set foot in the Baptist church again. As far as he could tell, Gilchrist's reputation stood no worse off afterward than before that Monday in October in the back room of the mission. In fact, leaving town probably increased her popularity tremendously. One of the last public words Sam heard about Gini supported this notion. He overheard two women, who, he knew, had disliked Gini, in the drugstore one day. "Oh, they'll be leaving next week. The going-away social is this Sunday night," one of the women said. The other: "And they've only been here a few months? My, I hate to see them leave. Gini was such a hard worker. I loved her to death."

Sam Warren had nothing to say to anyone about Gini. He never forgot her, and he never fell in love again.

Now, at seventy-three years old, Sam was mostly content with his life -- save for one small goal he still had to accomplish. He had succeeded in every business venture he had entered: He owned ten pool halls, six liquor stores, piddled in bets on college football and held interest in prostitution through escort services in Tallahassee, Jacksonville and other Florida cities. There was one thing he had been slow on, too slow, and, consequently, he lagged in sharing the phenomenal cash flow associated with it. His drug trade had been a timid sideline thus far, some pot and crack sales to college kids and people in the poor neighborhoods like the one around the old Riverton high school. Drug operations had spread across South Georgia and North Florida in the 1970s and '80s. Now, the outside crack trade was moving in on his market, and he couldn't hold back any longer. He was ready to grow this business, take control of his own territory, and branch out into others'. He had planned this next move, except for two prickly details. He couldn't account for a significant amount of the crack Louie Basford had been responsible for selling. It was gone; it must have been sold. He had to deal with that little problem decisively, and soon. And then, there was the Schoolhouse Man himself. Renovating that old building, shit! Sam thought, seething in his living room. Too close to the trade. Too close.

He was about to make a trip to Florida. When he returned to Riverton, he would set about trying to solve his mystery of the misplaced crack cocaine and stolen money, and find out who might be in with Louie, poor dumb, stupid Louie, on this diversion of Sam Warren's property. Sam had slipped on that one, but not to worry. Uncle Sam would take care of things. The schoolhouse, that rundown old building people called Graystone High, was not going to be turned into any fancy offices. It would be better for all, Sam reasoned, if the Atlanta boy were out of the picture. How would he do that? He hoped Louie's demise would help.

Sam sat butt naked in his easy chair, his farmhouse living room littered with newspapers, Kentucky Fried Chicken boxes and beer cans.

He called out to the bedroom -- or wherever that gal was. "Tootsie!" he shouted. "Get your ass in here and bring that other bitch wid you."

Tootsie walked into the room. She was nude.

"Yeah, Sam?"

"Where is she?"

"Yowanda's taking a shower. I'm next."

"You all get packed. We're going down south. But, wait. Come here..."

Tootsie danced over to the chair and sat on the arm. She looked down at Sam, who had taken out his dentures and was grinning at her. She could see he was ready. She knew what to do before rushing Yowanda out of the shower to start packing.

She kneeled down next to Sam Warren. He grinned at her, sat back and tried for the life of him to relax. Soon, he did.

Chapter 5 - The Web

Louie Basford's first mistake was taking a hundred-dollar bill out of the register and tucking it into his pocket two years previous. Had he stopped at that, things might have passed without notice. But he didn't. He couldn't. Next, about a week after the hundred, he slipped two twenties into his double-knit trousers after closing one night. A week later, on three separate occasions, he took several tens to buy cigarettes, girlie magazines and other items. Eventually, as a matter of course, he was taking thirty or forty dollars, sometimes all on the same day.

The hundred had been special. In all his years working for the Boss, he had never had a hundred-dollar bill. He held on to it, never considering putting it back, although he spent the rest of the money most eagerly.

Carlton Webber had brought the bill in one day, having acquired it selling non-tax whiskey in Madison, Florida. Webber managed pretty well in selling some twenty cases and had been paid off in hundreds. He dropped by the pool hall and got Louie to cash one of the bills.

For Louie, the cash register and the envelope he kept in the back of the register's drawer became additional income in just a few short weeks. He was dumbfounded that he had never thought of it before. In all, he probably took out about a thousand dollars, a considerable amount of money for Louie. He had found what he thought of as an easily accessible income enhancement. Yep. Income enhancement. He smiled at this little joke. In most ways, Louie was no different than many unscrupulous employees of small businesses who found that cash registers and brown, greasy, wrinkled envelopes in top desk drawers were easy sources of extra money. The difference was that those folks didn't work for Sam Warren.

Louie's second blunder -- taking money on a regular basis -- became a new habit that cost him his life. By taking the money day in, day out, no matter how insignificant to the pool hall's receipts, Louie was establishing a pattern. It was inevitable that Sam Warren would suspect something. Sam may not have found out about the hundred, but after a while he would figure out a shortfall existed, start snooping around and find out who took the money that belonged to Sam Warren, one of the cagiest and cruelest businessmen in South Georgia. He ran legitimate businesses and managed a number of illegal rackets for years. He had never been arrested.

The nickel-and-dime cash withdrawals had given Louie a false sense of confidence. So several months after he took the hundred, when he was moved from the pool room to another job for Sam Warren, Louie was set to adapt his skills of diversion to his new assignment: Managing Sam's small-time crack cocaine sales in Riverton's poor neighborhoods. There was little to skim here, but over time, and in just a few months, Louie managed to divert and stow away several bags of crack in a place not even Sam Warren was likely to find it -- safely hidden in a "pile of rags," Louie told himself, again laughing at his humor. Eventually, at a time Louie hadn't really thought about, he would sell his little cache and, well, he just might retire.

This was Louie's last mistake, and the fatal one. Louie, of course, had made mistakes all his life. Sam Warren never did. Until Louie. Louie Basford was Sam Warren's first big mistake, and one of his last.

Louie had been working for Sam Warren twelve years when Carlton Webber walked into the pool hall that October afternoon, ordered a Pabst high-top and handed Louie the hundred for the beer with a casual, "'Fraid that's all I got." Carlton looked lean and cool in his white T-shirt, windbreaker, blue jeans and brogans. Brown hair trimmed close. Arms muscular. Lips tight like the Marine he had been. Carlton was confident and friendly. Louie, in contrast, always seemed pale, even in the dimly lit pool hall. He sat in the pool hall day and night. He greased down his hair too much and wore loose shirts, usually short sleeves with squaretails hanging out, and baggy double-knit trousers. His watch, when he wore one, dangled around a flimsy wrist. Thin and always appearing weak, he hunched slightly. Most any day, any season, he looked as if he were drying out from a hard sweat or recovering from a bout of pneumonia. He looked at you through squinty eyes that would open wide to his other expression, one of exaggerated amazement. Mostly, though, Louie tried in vain to make jokes and partake in pool hall chatter. At this he always failed, and eventually he would shut up, sit behind the bar, serve beer and pickled eggs, make change, and sweep up afterward. He didn't care for beer, but he loved good bourbon and took several drinks after getting home from the pool hall every night.

"Say, bud, I brought you something in the car," Carlton Webber told Louie after counting out his change.

Louie looked up, eyes squinting.

"Let me fetch it." Carlton returned with a brown bag. From it he pulled a half-gallon bottle of Kentucky Home bourbon. "See, I remembered you."

Louie thanked him wide-eyed: "Sure will enjoy this, yessir, Carl. Sure do thank you." He thought that an appropriately gracious remark, so he repeated it.

"Nothing, Louie. Nothing t'all." Carlton finished his beer and left. Louie did appreciate the bourbon, but his thoughts froze on the hundred-dollar bill, which he slipped in his pants pocket. Before he could retire to the ice tea glass full of Carlton's present that evening, Louie had to lock up and hand in an account slip and cash bag to Sam Warren, as he did every night. That night, the night he took the hundred, Louie gave no worry to the missing money. He handed Sam the bag without any thought of what he had done.

Three months later, on a Wednesday night, Sam Warren asked Louie to meet him at the old high school. Louie took off most Wednesday evenings when Bennie Barfield was there to run the pool hall. Louie went thinking the Boss had chosen him for something, perhaps a role in another new venture the older man always referred to but never seemed to move on. Louie thought he was important, a final delusion to a sour life and one of no importance at all.

Sam Warren left the school in his truck. He drove the pickup because he usually used it only on the farm, thus he likely would not be recognized while driving it in town. Tonight's mission had been planned and carried out carefully. He knew it was Louie's night off, and when he called Louie late in the afternoon, he warned him not to tell a soul about the meeting. He told Louie it was a confidential meeting on an important matter, and he hinted that someone important would be present. Louie assumed he would be a minor player at the meeting, but a trusted and valued participant, no less.

While Louie's crime wave seemed small and insignificant compared to the range of possibilities, to Sam Warren it was grand theft, particularly since he was certain Louie also had been diverting some of the Boss's drugs -- and Sam assumed, selling elsewhere for Louie's own profit. Sam was outraged. But he rarely showed his anger publicly and would not in this case; he would simply get even. Later, he would work out his rage in other pursuits.

After taking care of Louie and leaving him at the old school, Sam Warren drove back roads to the farm. He called Bennie Barfield around eleven, just as the pool hall was closing, to tell Barfield he was in Tallahassee and would be out of town several days. He instructed Barfield to deposit the pool hall cash at the bank. Bennie Barfield could be trusted since he was, unlike Louie, too smart to fool with Sam's money. Too smart, perhaps, Sam often thought. At the farm, he parked the truck, got into his big Cadillac and drove toward Madison. He passed through the town and headed west on Interstate 10 to Tallahassee. The tall shoulder grass bent in the night as the big Cadillac swooshed past at ninety miles an hour. Just after midnight he rolled through Tallahassee on the Apalachee Parkway, stopped at an intersection near the Capitol and turned onto Monroe Street. He rolled through the south of town, staying within the speed limit and easing up slowly to every traffic light. He picked up speed at a crossroads on the city's outskirts and ran a red light. No one around him. He moved fast into the blackness of pine forests. He picked up the mobile phone receiver and, holding the receiver against the backdrop of the Cadillac's instrument panel and dialing the number.

A woman's voice answered, and it wasn't sleepy: "947-2286."

"Who the hell's this?"

"Might I ask the same, sir?"

Sam Warren laughed into the receiver.

"You must be one of Charlotte's new ones. She there? Tell her Sambo's a-callin'."

"Yeah."

Charlotte picked up in a few seconds.

"Sambo?"

"It's me, baby."

"Where in hell are you calling from? You in Riverton or your Cadillac somewhere, cruising for young girls?"

"Daddy's comin' home, bay-bee."

"When is he getting here?"

"I'd say in about half an hour. I would have said that. In Tallahassee. But right now, I'm hitting eighty-five headin' south of town. Be in Crawfordville in about five minutes. And your place in another twenty or so."

"Shit, Sam. Why do you do this to me? I got five legislators down here tonight. They still hootin' and hollerin', drunk as hell, and I'm short on help."

"Stop your moaning, woman. We'll stay in the trailer on the creek. Ain't Julie there?"

"Yeah, I reckon it's OK... Oh, hell, Sam, you're welcome anytime. Maybe these bastards will leave and not stay, anyway. One of 'ems so drunk he's done passed out, but not before puking his guts out. Another one's sleeping it off in the back of their limo."

"Sounds like pure hell."

"Well, come on anyway."

"Awright. Bye, hon'."

"See you soon, Sambo."

Sam replaced the phone in its dashboard cradle and looked out at a sign for Wakulla Springs. How many times had he been there, he thought. He remembered the glass-bottom boats and the young blonde sisters he had taken there in the late forties. Geena and Deena were their names. Though they were two years apart, but looked just alike. He remembered them vividly, two naive live wires. Young, pretty and full of life. His affections ended with Geena. Deena married a doctor and still lived in Albany, Georgia. Geena was killed in a car wreck in Montgomery, Alabama, in the late fifties. He remembered another time at Wakulla, a recent visit with Charlotte. They drove by the springs the day she first visited the lodge with a real estate agent.

Charlotte Welles ran one of the last old-time whorehouses near Florida's capital city. The building was once a hunting lodge, and now, for three months before the April opening of every Florida legislative session and a month or two after, she ran her business round the clock. Charlotte would then take the rest of the year off, usually fleeing to Cancun -- relaxing, not working. During the "seasonal" months, she worked hard at managing what seemed to visitors to be a traditional whorehouse. Actually, she described her business as a high-class companion service provided, for handsome fees, to dignitaries from the state capital, many of whom were legislators accepting favors from lobbyists, trading favors with one another, or, through the resources of special-interest groups, paying back favors, or merely riding whatever special interest coattail they could to advance their own political futures, financial riches and personal gratification.

Charlotte performed well in what she did, as, in her own

words, a "hostess." Her girls stayed healthy and gorgeous, and any one of them could command one or two thousand dollars a night in New York or Europe. Rated Grade A as call girls, not mere hookers, these women had never flagged a car on a street corner -- nor would they be caught dead working the yellow pages listings for escort services.

Charlotte's house sat on the edge of the Apalachicola National Forest. Most people in Tallahassee who knew about such things called the place Charlotte's Web. It was located two miles off a graded forest service road, so deep in the piney woods you had to look carefully to catch the turnoff onto a road more like a hog trail than a driveway. The marker that guided men to Charlotte's hearth was a black mailbox with a white spider's web painted on it. When most men saw the mailbox and its logo, their hearts fluttered, and they felt a sensation unlike no other.

State Rep. Frederick Simpson curled up in the back on the white limousine parked in front of the hunting lodge. He felt awful. He was a good boy in the capital city, but away from Tallahassee on legislative junkets and cruises with friends, he acted naughty, naughty, naughty. This trip had not interested him much, anyway. The pork barrel rednecks in the lodge, pawing the girls and drinking scotch, as he had done early on, had sided with him in planning legislation to encourage industrial development in several of Florida's poorer northern counties, most of which made up his and the rednecks' districts. The lobbyists putting on the party represented companies that could benefit from the development bill, should it be structured and passed with the right language. They sought favors, and here, deep in woods joining the Panhandle with the rest of Florida, they rapidly secured what they needed.

He found the limo's plush back seat as comfortable and roomy as a soft bed. He dozed, then jerked awake in restless sleep. Inside, the party went on, unheard by him.

Frederick Simpson, small-town Georgia boy making good in the Sunshine State, honors graduate from Emory University, Law Review at Yale, senior partner in a big Jacksonville law firm, now a converted and bona fide Florida citizen. With all that and the backing of several Jacksonville businessmen, he had gained entry to the Legislature and now, eight years later, he was trying to get some sleep in the back seat of a limousine while several of his committee colleagues partied and whored it up inside an erstwhile hunting lodge south of Tallahassee.

The lobbyists truly thought Simpson had caught a bug or consumed too much liquor too soon. Why else would a red-blooded single man sit out the evening chill in a limo, when he could be cuddled up with one of the finest looking women in the state? Belch Allen, the senior lobbyist, walked out to the car twice to check on Frederick. The second time, Belch looked into the rear window and saw Frederick sleeping. He walked back inside, shaking his head at these part-time lawyers, sometime legislators who couldn't hold their liquor.

But Allen had no idea of the real reason Simpson had retired to the limo. While he had tipped the bottle a little too much, the truth was he could care less about the ravishing females at the lodge. Frederick Simpson preferred other delights. As he drifted into fitful sleep, he longed for his hotel suite and the young Florida State fraternity brother who often shared his bed.

Twenty-three minutes after setting down the phone receiver, Sam Warren pulled in behind the limo in front of Charlotte's Web. He idled the engine for a moment, had second thoughts, and wheeled around to the lodge's side entrance at the kitchen. It looked as if every light in the lodge were on. He waited a moment and listened, but heard nothing of the earlier ruckus.

Sam walked into the kitchen, looked around, and through an open door saw Nellie, Charlotte's maid, asleep in an old recliner in her television room behind the pantry. Nellie often dropped off to sleep after serving the food, cleaning up the dishes, and seeing the party move in other directions. Miss Charlotte had not served a meal that night, and the men seemed more interested in the liquor and elegant munchies than the girls, so Nellie had been kept busy later than usual. Miss Charlotte finally closed down the snack service after one of the men got sick and sloshed the hallway bathroom with several loads of vomit. Such was life in a whorehouse, Nellie thought as she cleaned up the mess. Nellie minced no words, at least in her mind, about the hunting lodge known as Charlotte's Web: A whorehouse it was, pure and simple.

Nellie woke up, sensing someone looking at her. There he was, Mr. Sam Warren from up in Georgia. Come down here for a little relaxation with Miss Charlotte and maybe pick out a new girl, and look what he finds. A bunch of drunk politicians hollering and tellin' awful jokes and rubbing their hands all over the girls.

"Nellie, you ready to put the lights out?" Mr. Sam said, his hand resting on the light switch.

"Yassir," Nellie replied. Off went the lights and the door closed gently as she turned back over in the worn recliner and tried to go back to sleep. The noise in the big room began to subside. One or two couples had retired to the small bedrooms on the other end of the building. Nellie, like Frederick Simpson, darted in and out of sleep. Now she was ready to slip off for several hours. That she did.

Sam Warren knew nothing of Nellie's thoughts. He never considered what she might think of this place, her work place. He walked across the large kitchen to the refrigerator and poked through it for a Coke. He found a blue-label bottle of club soda, closed the refrigerator door and opened the cabinet containing a royal supply of liquor. He picked out an open bottle of Talisker single malt and poured it in a tumbler. He threw in two cubes of ice and doused all with the club soda.

He enjoyed drinking scotch late at night, although he otherwise preferred beer or bourbon, or whenever he was bothered by something and had to think. He had not bargained on Charlotte's being this busy. Hell, the Legislature convened more than two months from now. What were these people, workaholics? Having to do away with Louie had disturbed him, and especially so the way it turned out. Sam had gone emotional at the end, erupting in near madness at the thought of what happened to him in that teacher's lounge years before. What the hell, Sam thought, got it behind you, now don't fret over it. Shooting Louie at the school was sloppy and risky, considering the Atlanta boy could have come back from his girl friend's any time. He hadn't, Sam reasoned. No car and no sign of him all evening. He took a long draw from the glass and felt better. The shooting would leave a message and it might accomplish what Sam hoped: Scare that fellow into abandoning his plans for an office renovation or kindergarten or whatever he was doing with the building. These high-flying, big-city investors, Sam thought, how in hell did they find Riverton, anyway? Usually, a few days with a woman like Charlotte, who possessed wonderfully full breasts and endless energy in bed and whose talk invigorated, gave him time to relax and run things through his mind.

"They're all taken care of, I think," Charlotte said, standing in the kitchen's double doorway leading to the lodge's dining area. Her voice sounded soft and Southern, but always determined. "Thank the Lord that good-looking Jacksonville lawyer got sick or else old Char would've had to slip into a black teddy and entertain him. Not that I'd mind that. Right, Sambo?"

Sam turned around and looked at dark curls falling around Charlotte's head. She had dressed in a black leather mini skirt and low-cut, red sleeveless pullover V-neck sweater. The V dipped deeply into cleavage, and nipples poked their pointed firmness through the wooly knit. Black stockings -- Sam knew them to be hooked to a garter belt --

stretched over shapely legs. Shoes matched the sweater's red.

"Yep, hon'. You right about that," he said. "I just imagine you would enjoy it. Now come over here and give Sambo a kiss."

She did just that, striding across the kitchen floor, kicking off the red shoes, one hitting the refrigerator, the other landing near the gas range. She embraced him first, then leaned back and looked up at him. Then she reached up and kissed old Sam Warren smack on the lips, firmly and deeply.

"Mmm. Law, that's mighty fine," Sam said, holding strong, veined hands around Charlotte's narrow, tight waist. A finger played with the sweater's back, eased up behind the red wool and moved down the mini skirt's waistband. He fondled a zipper tab but let it stay put.

"Sounds like you got the Boy Scouts tucked in. Ready to go to the creek for a serious party?"

"Almost. Not quite." She nudged her nose into his neck, moved down the front of his open white shirt and licked his gray chest hairs. "'Bout time for Julie to excuse herself and come down. Told her we'd talk before I left. Then we can slip out of here."

Sam looked thoughtful, and Charlotte asked what about.

"How much do I get for all this trouble, anyway?"

"The usually split at the end of the quarter, mister serious businessman." She let go and stooped to pick up her shoes.

"Still cold outside?"

"Chilly. Not bad, but take a coat."

"Oh... All right. Let me go get that and some other things. Make yourself comfy. I'll be right back."

Sam freshened his drink. Charlotte took longer than he expected. When she returned she had on a full-length fur, a small night bag and a plastic sack with champagne and some boxes in it. The hose had disappeared, he noticed. White and natural, her legs held their appeal.

"Let's go, Sambo," she said as she managed her

possessions and opened the kitchen door.

"You set with Julie, now?"

"Oh, yeah. Let's go."

Charlotte hopped in and snuggled up to Sam as the Cadillac's engine roared. He slapped the automatic gearshift in reverse, wheeled out of the kitchen parking spot, turned around, and took off down the narrow dirt driveway. Sam felt better. The drink helped, and Charlotte did her part as earlier events of the night left his mind.

The creek-side mobile home was three miles away. Near the forest service road, Charlotte switched on the dome light.

"Like my new fur?"

"Who gave you that?"

"Belch Allen, one of the lobbyists here tonight. Kind of a pre-legislative session surprise."

"Man has shit for a name, but good taste."

"He does, doesn't he?"

With the inside light on, Sam could hardly see to maneuver the narrow drive. He looked at Charlotte, saw her smiling up at him, watched her soft hands part the fur coat, flinging one side across the passenger seat and wedging the other beside his leg. A white knee cocked, a foot moved up to rest on the seat, and Sam Warren beheld the fair nakedness of a most beautiful woman.

Chapter 6 - Memories

Brooks felt tired when the sheriff, his deputies and Dub Campbell left the schoolhouse around five o'clock that morning. He couldn't think about going to sleep, but he lay down on the bed anyway. He was glad to see a friend from long ago, but they'd had little time to talk. The sheriff kept to business, had gone over Brooks' story repeatedly while the deputies gathered evidence and made photographs upstairs and down. Dub hadn't said much, other than to acknowledge he had known the younger Brooks and was pleased to see him again.

The two had attended the same summer camp one year, Brooks as a camper and Dub, then a college student, as a counselor. Although Brooks was much younger than Dub, the two became close friends and were a well known duo at the camp, matching quick wits and the free spirit of Georgia boys in jokes and pranks on other campers. Dub, the big, good-looking football player at the University of Georgia, symbolized everything that Brooks, then a rising eleventh-grader, desired to become.

Brooks wanted to talk about that summer, find out what Dub had been doing since then, and about Riverton, the town that gave both of them some common ties and the place that brought them together again. He lay in bed, restless from lack of sleep, eyes looking up at the ceiling, then blinking heavily, eventually closing and allowing him to drift, only to jolt awake. Finally, he slept for several hours, aroused occasionally by barking noises, a cadence of thumps and bumps and the splash of blood against a wall, a sound similar to someone slapping a wet mop on a hard, concrete floor.

He woke up at two o'clock that afternoon and realized he couldn't shake the dream: Dogs really were barking outside his window. He sat on the bed's edge for a few minutes before standing up and walking through the dark hall and up the steps to the bathroom. There, standing in the cold room over a washbasin, he stripped off his shirt and drenched his head and upper body with water and soap, rinsing off quickly and groping for a towel. Back in the room, shivering, he combed his hair, put on deodorant and a clean shirt, grabbed his jacket and walked out the room's outside door.

Then he remembered he had left his car at Sara's two nights ago. It wouldn't start, and he meant to call a mechanic. Now, he would have to walk to Houston Avenue, to Sara's big white house.

He told Sara everything that happened the night before. When he got to the part about riding with the body to the hospital, she left the room to fix him and herself tumblers of bourbon and water.

"Who... what... How do they think it happened?" she said, holding out the drink glass, no ice.

"They're not saying much. Rather the sheriff isn't saying much," Brooks said. "Funny, his deputies are just sort of there. They contributed nothing, really other than taking a few pictures and poking around the building. He didn't seem interested in consulting them or bringing them in on his own thoughts, although he wouldn't have done that in front of me, anyway."

"So, you think they suspect you?"

"Nobody said anything, but it's clear they are puzzled about why I was there. Yeah, they may think I could have done it, even though they didn't arrest me. They just told me not to leave town, but I'm kind of surprised I'm not sitting over there in the jail right now. They seem to focus on the circumstantial and the easiest way to solve a crime. I don't know, really."

Sara held her glass and sat down on the arm of Brooks' chair. Clearly, Brooks was worried, but she thought he was touched by something other than the shooting.

"It's been a tough night and day for you, hasn't it?" she

said.

Brooks looked up at her. He needed this wonderful woman. She understood him and sympathized with him. But he also needed to talk with his Atlanta psychotherapist, Dr. Harriet Browning. Sara substituted for Harriet in some ways, but they were so different he could not imagine simply replacing one with the other. He turned away from her to sip the bourbon and stared into the intricate designs of the living room rug.

He had not talked to Harriet in several months. His leaving Atlanta had upset her orderly world, and he felt bad about that. She had said little when he actually left, but he knew his move hurt her. Harriet expressed hurt only once, years ago, in Washington. That hot shot. Who was it? Oh yeah, Stratford Willis, Virginian, socialite, snob. Since Stratford Willis, Harriet had shut her emotions deep inside, saving the one breakdown on the sofa with Brooks after his wife died. They had needed each other then. Now, what had he done? He had left her, wide open and alone. He felt bad, and the hurt was growing. He couldn't sit here with Sara much longer. He would have to leave, go call Harriet, go running back to fulfill his own yearning and his need to be healed in some way. Dr. Harriet, physician to the poor, diseased, dysfunctional Brooks Sheffield: His surrogate mother, his lover, his healer. Who healed Harriet, Brooks? Who put their arms around her at winter's end and held her while she cried her eyes out upon your abrupt departure? These thoughts humiliated him.

"Brooks, what's wrong?" Sara was stroking his neck and leaning into him the way she had that night on her front porch. Soothing Sara. Healing Harriet.

"I guess it's all too much for me, though I don't know why I'm telling you this," he said, turning his face into her breast. He kissed her there, on the breast, his lips lightly touching it through her dress.

"I love you, Brooks."

"Oh, Sara. I ought to say that to you. I do love you. I

will. But it's hard. Life's such a sad, tragic thing, and there's really so much you don't understand about me. Love is so hard to say, sometimes."

"But I love you, anyway."

He said nothing. He let her take his head in her arms and he let her massage his head, weaving fingers through his short hair, and he eased up as she worked those strong basketball hands down his neck and down around his shoulder blades. All this time they sat without talking and let their eyes and thoughts drift into the haze taking over the day and the room.

The doorbell jolted their mood. Sara walked to the front of the house. Brooks listened as voices muttered through the long front hall and at the door. Then he heard footsteps on the old oak floor and Sara's inviting voice.

"Come on back," she said to someone. "He's right here in the living room."

The door opened and Dub Campbell walked in.

"Hello, cowboy," he said with a grin Brooks remembered well, though he had not seen it in a long time.

"Dub Campbell. Sorry we had to meet again with this kind of stuff going on."

"What stuff is that? The shooting?"

"Well, for me, at least, this isn't exactly an everyday occurrence."

"Heck, what you worried about boy?"

"Come on. You know Johnson thinks I did it. Tell me, why didn't you all arrest me right there on the spot?"

"You?"

"Yeah, me."

Then the old Dub Campbell stepped forth in that big, boisterous, confident laugh of his.

"Hell, Brooks," he said. "You didn't do it. We know that much. Don't think the sheriff has any serious thoughts along those lines, either. Least not by what he's telling me. You quit your agonizing, and let's go get us a beer. Don't think I've ever been more surprised than when I walked in that school and saw you."

Brooks looked at Sara, standing in the doorway.

"You all can stay here. I got plenty of beer and other things," she said. "Or maybe you boys want to talk by yourselves. That's OK, too. I understand."

"No, ma'am," Dub said. "In fact, I won't take him if you don't come. I've got a great place for you two. Brooks, bet you haven't seen it, being Baptist and all. We might even shed some light on this shooting business. And if we don't, hell, we'll get drunk anyway."

"Oh, no. You all go ahead," Sara said. "I'm not one to stand in the way of male bonding."

"Nope," Brooks said. "You're coming."

Dub cocked his head and looked whimsically at Sara, his baldhead wrinkled, his eyes wide open.

"Please allow me, an overweight, burnt out Georgia flatfoot who drinks too much, the enormous pleasure of being seen in public drinking beer with you. Please, indulge me, beautiful lady."

"Who could resist that? Brooks, you can just stay here. Dub and I will do the bonding!" Sara said, teasingly grabbing Brooks' arm and pulling him through the door only to stop at the front of the house and begged time to change into a skirt and sweater and fluff her hair. She emerged from the upstairs bathroom adorned in bright red lipstick, red enough, Dub thought, for the place he was taking them: The Starlite Lounge and Dance Hall on the Florida line south of Riverton.

All three piled into the front seat of Dub's car, Sara bending her legs around radio equipment that crowded the middle floorboard. As she scooted over in the seat, she landed on something hard -- Dub's state-issue pistol.

"I feel like I'm on a college trip to the beach," she said. "This gun reminds me of compulsory necking, in which the girl is forever condemned to sore buns because she has to sit as close to the boy as possible, and usually on the brake handle, no matter the discomfort or personal injury."

"Well, sorry, my dear lady," Dub said. "But I spent a

summer with Joe Ree over there and I found out then not to bend over in the shower with him, let alone allow him in the love seat. You'll have to be uncomfortable or sit in the back."

Sara laughed. "Well, there is another alternative, you know?"

"What might that be?"

"You could sit in the back."

"Brooks and I are bonding, remember?"

"Well, then, I'll drive and you both can sit in the back," Sara offered.

"You always did settle on the smart, libber types, Brooks. Whatever got into you, boy? Although I will say this one has the looks that will overcome any drawbacks her notions might present."

"Guess I'm just open minded, that's all," he replied.

"Damn South Georgia liberal," Dub said. "You one of a kind, boy, I will say that."

"He's a good man, Brooks," Sara said to Dub. She squeezed Brooks' knee lovingly as Dub started the car.

Dub drove south out of town, and the banter went on and on. Sara laughed. Dub was happy. Brooks wondered if he was really out of a big mess. He doubted it.

Brooks' father would have called The Starlite Lounge a juke joint, the roadhouse of the region that combined poolroom with dance hall and held a few tables for talking and drinking. The main building was concrete block with a sheet-metal addition tacked on in back, one that looked like a modern farm building. Windowless, save for one up next to the front door, the building inside was dark. The front part of the building served as a beer hall, the back holding pool and snooker tables. Several people, mostly men, hovered around and over the pool tables. Shots popped. Heads nodded. Beer bottles turned up often over sucking mouths.

If unpainted concrete and metal walls boasted the usual neon beer signs, calendars and little else, the ceiling was incredible to behold. From every inch of it hung what the bartender and a flashing sign out front purported to be the world's largest collection of redneck memorabilia: more than 2,500 baseball caps, with the gallery ever expanding. And all these caps had a message to convey that spoke louder than any major league team, for as the true icons of redneck country these promoted farm implements, fertilizer, chicken, baseball teams, chewing tobacco, snuff, Gulf Coast beaches and, of course, sex, all in a manner some might consider in poor taste, even obscene, although none of the Starlite's customers ever complained.

The bartender and regulars spotted Sara and Brooks as newcomers immediately because they looked skyward reading the labels, patches, logos and suggestions on all the caps.

One cap proclaimed simply, "Panama City Beach, Florida," and along with its variations dominated the "places" category. Another read: "Hahira Polo Club." Others were less buoyant about Georgia towns and cities: "Atlanta: (Arm) Pit of the Peach Sate," rivaled only by its cousin, "Ludowici: Speed Trap to the World."

Variations on "Georgia Bulldogs" made this cap supreme among the college logos, even including one wooly said to have been worn by legendary Georgia coach Wally Butts. Its faded, moth-eaten beige surface sported a dark red "G" on its crown.

A poultry processor's "Young and Tender Chicken" cap looked as if it had been drenched in boiling grease then hung up to dry. The cap nearly dripped of the human sweat that stained every fiber and washed the bill from what once was a bright yellow to a filthy, muted orange.

Ford logos won the vehicle division, hands down. One cap depicted the "Big Foot" four-wheel-drive champ, and another declared irreverently, "F.O.R.D. -- Fix Or Repair Daily."

Several Atlanta Braves and Falcons caps dangled alongside other professional sports teams, even one New Orleans Saints cap. But sports clearly fell short of the main topic catching most people's eye and sparking their comments. These were the naughty caps, most portraying shapely females or funny -- Sara would have said sexist -- sayings about women, or both.

The one Brooks howled about said: "Life's a Bitch... And Then I Married One."

Another turned the tables on the guys, and it caught Sara's glance: "The More I Learn About Men, The More I Love My Volkswagen."

As Brooks walked over to the bar, Dub pointed out the ones he thought Sara might have missed.

"Look over there," he said, leaning over and putting his arm around her shoulder. "You can't really see it. Look right there." He pointed to a cap several tables over, which said: "Nurses Love Little Pricks."

Sara chuckled in a low voice. Brooks sat down beside them with three beers.

Dub pointed just above Brooks' head to a cap that appeared to be covered in droppings from a very large bird, perhaps a pelican. The cap's patch stated forlornly: "We Could Be Touring Europe, But My Wife Insisted on Daytona Beach."

"This is some tourist spot itself, Dub," he said. "How on earth did you every find it?"

"It's on my regular rounds. Hell, boy. These are my kind of people. You'll like 'em, too," he said, winking at Sara and looking around at the collection of mill workers, farm boys and, Dub knew, some troublemakers who had jail records.

"Oh, well, I suppose this has some cultural meaning."

"Keep cool, buddy. Just sit back, sip on a beer or two. Enjoy your lady. We got a lot of catching up to do." Dub rocked back on his chair. Someone dropped coins into a jukebox and a Bonnie Raitt song throbbed through the lounge.

As talk of baseball caps ebbed, the two men dove into how they met. Dub and Brooks traded anecdotes as if they were telling Sara bedtime stories. The tale never ended, rather it leapt from one jocular slight to another.

Dub excused himself to go to the bathroom. On the way, Brooks noticed, he stopped briefly to talk to the bartender, who shook his head at whatever question Dub had asked. Brooks glanced into the back of the room, toward the pool tables and the movement around them, sipping his beer, slipping again into the muddle of the last eighteen hours. Sara caught his eye and demanded his attention by scooting her chair closer to his and rubbing her bare knees into his leg.

"Hey! If you don't dance with me, Dub will. You better watch it, or he might snatch me away."

"You'd let him, too," Brooks said, still looking into the back. Then he caught her point and paid her some attention: "I thought you were a liberated woman, anyway, not allowing any man to pick or choose you?"

"All men, no. Some men, yes. You're the man. Dance with me now, and I'll show you."

"Come on, Sara. This isn't a dance hall. Besides, you're the only woman here. If we start dancing, every man in the place will want to cut in and keep you going all night."

Dub rounded the corner from the back tugging up on his fly, leaning forward to check for drip spots and heading back to the table.

"You two lovebirds better watch it. This place ain't the senior prom. You don't want to be giving these fellows any ideas the woman's easy, Brooks."

"If she's in here with you, they probably already figure that. What the hell have you been doing the last twenty some odd years anyway, Dubya Dee?"

"Failing." Dub answered quickly, but he didn't seem to be joking.

"No, really. You mentioned a daughter earlier. She around here?"

"The only thing I have in common with my daughter, besides blood, is we both graduated from the University of Georgia. That's about it. I haven't talked with Janice in two years. She doesn't come to see me and has never invited me to visit her in Chicago, not that I'd go."

"You would," Sara assured.

Dub studied the idea.

"No," he said. "We just don't get along. Don't know what it is. I guess the divorce came at a bad time, when Janice was fifteen. She visited with me until she went to college, but then I lost her. Never went to Athens, never took her to a Bulldog game or anything. It was a tough time for her. And it was real tough for me. You know, I wanted to take her to some games, tell her about the good old days when I was playing ball, living in Reed Hall and making like big man on campus. But her mother got married within a year after we divorced and moved to South Carolina. Janny was taken right into that family. Graduated from high school up there. I suppose it was a better substitute than having a part-time father, which I was most of the time."

"Man, you're hard on yourself," Sara said. "From all I've heard you two say, you can't be such a bad guy. Especially if this wonderful man likes you." She leaned across and put her arms around Brooks' round shoulders, pulled him to her and kissed his right ear.

"Him? Likes me?" Dub asked. "Hell, he used to worship me."

"Is that right?" Sara asked Brooks.

"Like dog worships man."

"You know, there's one story you haven't told her, at least not this evening," Dub reminded Brooks.

"I'm afraid to ask which one," Brooks said.

Then Dub turned to Sara. "Listen," he said. "I don't know how much he's told you about his past. But did he ever mention the lie that he once attended Wake Forest University?"

"No, but he's gone over everything else about his youth," she said, pinching Brooks' leg under the table.

Brooks just shook his head, knowing what was coming.

"Well, we met at a boys camp, Camp Wakonda, up near

Black Mountain, North Carolina. He was in high school then. A Baptist camp, but they even let Episcopalians like me work there, long as you were a jock in good standing."

"But he had to go to morning vespers down at the lake chapel, too," Brooks chimed in, "and one week he had to lead the singing. Boy, that woke everybody up!"

Sara laughed at the vision of Dub Campbell leading a bunch of sleepy-eyed boys, voices cracking, in singing Baptist hymns beside a lake in North Carolina.

"Anyhoo, he hung around after camp was over, he loved me so much," Dub went on. "So, I decided to fix him up with a date, and a college girl at that."

Brooks moaned.

"She was what, a sophomore at Wake Forest and you didn't know it?"

"No. She'd just graduated from high school," Brooks said.

"We dreamed up this tale that Brooks was a junior at Wake Forest, and hell, you'd never even set foot on the campus. He was scareder'n a cat hanging over water when he found out she was headin' to school over there in the fall. Oh, she asked him all kinds of questions about Wake Forest. He faked it pretty well, though, convincing her he was pre-med. I think she held his hand once and kissed him good night."

"You didn't do too badly yourself, as I recall."

"No. She was Susan. Susan Giles," Dub said, his mood shifting with the thought. "She was a humdinger. Went to Duke. Married a doctor."

"Dub, who's got your attention now?" Sara asked.

"Oh, I haven't been socializing much. Not since Gladys Mitchell sold her father's insurance company and took a job at one of the big company's down in Jacksonville."

"You went out with little Gladys Mitchell?" Brooks asked.

"Yeah, we dated off and on for five or six years. And, she ain't so little any more, Brooks."

"Good Lord! You really rob the cradle, don't you?"

"Well, let's just say my tastes fall in the area of good-looking younger women."

"Let's see. She would be ten years younger than me."

"That's right," Dub said, cracking a wry smile. "In her early to middle thirties at the time."

"Gladys, as I recall, was quite attractive at a very young age," Sara said. "Wasn't she a beauty queen?"

"Yeah," Brooks said. "She won the miss fat cattle show title one year. How did you let her slip away?"

Dub shrugged. "We call each other occasionally. My job gets in the way of serious relationships sometimes. Hell, look what it did to my marriage."

The group grew silent.

Soon Dub broke the solemn mood with more about their boys' camp days, recounting most of the summer leading up to the infamous double date and repeating much, in the course of several more rounds of beer, of what had been tossed about earlier.

Sara listened intently, laughed heartily and often, and grew fond of both these two men who had strolled into her solitary life, until now absorbed in academic pursuits and distancing herself from her divorce and the tragedy she buried so deeply. Dub Campbell, too, had not been this happy in years. But for Brooks, on this evening, as he recalled the fun times in his life, the sadness welled up again.

Chapter 7 - Watt

Watson Jennings Miller IV -- most people called him Watt -- sat way back in his swivel chair, staring blankly at his roll top desk. The desk, to anyone serious about old furniture, would be a prize, with its smooth finish on decades-old cherry wood. To Watson Jennings Miller IV, it was part of the ambiance, which he mostly invented, of being a country newspaper editor. Owning the desk meant nothing to him; being a country editor, or pretending to be one, was everything. At least, at one time he had thought being a country editor would satisfy him. At that time, it was all he ever wanted to do. Now, he had second thoughts.

Watson Jennings Miller IV was editor of The Riverton Herald. A former schoolteacher and Peace Corps volunteer, Miller had good intentions about everything he did. He meant well, but he started things he never finished. His career meanderings led through a progressive state of discouragement, which now grew tiresome for his wife and strained the business relationship with his father, the money side of the newspaper venture.

Now this murder thing had come up and confounded Watson Jennings Miller IV more than any other story in his three years of newspapering: How do you report a heinous killing in a hometown newspaper?

This is what he pondered while staring at the roll top desk. Many Riverton residents had known Louis Basford, even though his importance to the community was relatively nil. Sheriff Johnson frustrated Watson Jennings Miller IV the most, for he still had not talked about the case, and when the sheriff went mum so did his deputies. So Miller could write little. The only thing he had to go on was that the victim was shot to death in the abandoned high school building. He knew who owned and lived in the school -- Brooks Sheffield, the man from whom his father, Watson Jennings Miller III, had bought the paper.

He sighed. I suppose I'll have to track Sheffield down and interview him. What a bother. All this for a story, and a nasty one too, when he could have gotten the details over the phone from the sheriff, had he been willing to talk. Miller would try the sheriff again later. It was now late Thursday afternoon, so he'd have to hustle to get something on the murder today and then be home in time for dinner with Jenny's parents, who were in town for the weekend. Hustle was foreign to the demeanor of Watson Jennings Miller IV, but he picked up a small notebook, put on his corduroy jacket and walked to the door. He nervously placed a blue ballpoint pen in his shirt pocket, and asked Mrs. Pinson, the newspaper's clerk, circulation director and ad salesperson, to lock up whenever she left. He reminded her, too, that Baker's Department Store was three months behind on its ad account and would she please, today, ask the store manager to write the paper a check. Chagrined, she nodded agreement to the instructions. The office's front door rattled as if the glass were falling out. He shut it, jumped into the small pickup truck, and drove out to the high school in hopes of finding Brooks Sheffield. He remembered he actually had planned to do a feature on Sheffield sometime, whenever he got around to it.

Watt pulled up to the school, didn't see Sheffield's blue Volvo but parked his pickup anyway. Then he got out and walked around the back of the school, peeking in windows, banging on doors and trying to draw Brooks' attention in case he was inside the building. Through a window near the southwest corner, he looked in to see a bedroom. He knocked on the nearby door, and waited a moment before banging his fist on it several times. No response. Damned. No luck here. Watt drove around town looking for the Volvo, an uncommon automobile in Riverton. He found it parked in front of a large house on North Houston Avenue. He got out and knocked on the door. No one home. He headed back to the office and called the sheriff's office again.

Jenny Willingham Miller, from Savannah, had wholeheartedly backed Watt's idea for getting into the newspaper business. She supported it for three reasons: First, it was a business above all else, and she had heard newspapers, even weeklies, could make money. Second, maybe it meant Watt would settle down, become less of a "do gooder," as her father put it, and mainstream himself into community leadership, which she badly wanted him to do. Third, her selfish reason was that she missed being the center of attention, and all the attention she required came with being the wife of a weekly newspaper editor.

Jenny missed Savannah, her friends and her social life. Her parent's occasional visits and her visits home gave her something of the status she left behind many years ago to marry a man who was constantly looking for something and never finding anything. She had admired this soul seeking at first. She regarded teaching as a noble profession, she told Watt while they were in college at Mercer, and when he signed up for the Peace Corps, she got real excited about living in India. Fortunately for her, Watt became disenchanted with rural Indian life even before she did, and back they came, to a small house in Alma, Georgia, easy visiting distance from Savannah, and to another job for Watt, as a chemistry teacher at the local high school. Then, after years of hoping and waiting for a promotion to principal that never happened, Watt struck upon the notion of journalism and becoming a "country editor."

Jenny's father, Jason Willingham, had laughed at this idea. "Where in hell does that boy get these things?" he had asked. "And who's going to loan him the money to buy a paper? I'm not."

"He's not asking you to, even though I would hope you might consider it seriously if he did," Jenny had said. "His father's going to go in with him."

"In with him? Has the man lost his mind?"

"No. It's a reasonable business venture."

"Shoot. Newspapers? They're dying out. People don't read any more. They watch television. What this boy ought to do is buy one of these small-town cable television franchises. Hell, I know a dentist and some lawyers over in Millen who'd sell. Be a gold mine. On cable, I would go in with him."

Jenny was caught on that one. For all her hoping, she knew Watt could care less about running a profitable business. He wanted the glory, the sex appeal, the feeling of doing something with the remnants of his youthful idealism, and running a country newspaper was his current matter of interest and the hope for fulfilling the dream, the terribly elusive dream.

"I don't think Watt wants to operate a cable television business." That was all she could say.

"Well. It would go. And I would help him. And we would all make money."

With that, the subject dropped. Her father's initial comic reaction and cutting comments about the newspaper idea eventually diminished into a shake of the head in disgust after he heard how badly the paper performed financially. Jason Willingham never harped on people. He stated his opinion when he wanted to, but he wouldn't harp. This didn't allay his bewilderment over his son-in-law's lack of direction or help his disappointment over the way his only daughter's life seemed to have stalled. He felt that Jenny didn't love Watt much anymore. And on this, at least in part, Jason Willingham was correct.

Now, with her parents here, the good news won out over Jenny's gloom on two fronts: She was pregnant, finally, and Watt seemed ready for another move. This time, she hoped, it would be to Savannah -- for good. This was conditional, of course. A baby meant Watt had to have a decent job, and with that he would have to get out of the newspaper's debt. Even though his father had bought the paper, sparing Watt the burden of outstanding bank loans, Watt had managed to run up a respectable amount of debt operating the place. His father wouldn't like this when he learned the full extent of loans Watt had taken out. In time, Watson Jennings Miller III would lose patience. Then Watt would be forced out of his dream job. And that could happen pretty soon, Jenny thought. The news about the baby was certain, but word about leaving Riverton would have to wait. She hoped she could persuade Watt to make the move -- to Savannah -- before the baby came. Tonight, at least, Jenny could tell her parents about the promise of their first grandchild. She wanted Watt there with her.

Jenny had dinner ready promptly at eight o'clock. At eight-fifteen the telephone rang: A call from Watt.

"Why on earth aren't you home? Mom and Dad are here and we're ready to sit down at the table. You know I wanted to tell them tonight," Jenny said, her voice rising at her husband's tardiness.

Watt said he would head home soon, but he probably wouldn't be there for another half hour or so. He urged her to wait and tell her parents after he got home. Jenny said they would go ahead and start dinner. She told her parents that Watt had to work on a big story and couldn't join them until later. They, of course, offered to wait and eat when Watt arrived, but Jenny said he had insisted (he hadn't) that they begin the meal without him. They ate.

Watt, all this time, sat staring now out of the big front window of the office. Earlier in the evening he again had picked up the phone and called the courthouse, not expecting to get the sheriff on the line but trying, nevertheless, to get something for a story.

"Is the sheriff in?"

"Who's this?" The deputy wanted to know.

"Watson Miller at the paper."

"Hold on."

A hand cupped the receiver but Watt could hear muffled conversation.

"It's... newspaper editor..."

"Aw, hell," someone said from a distance in the room, "...don't want to talk to any news reporters... tell him..."

"He called all afternoon."

A minute more passed, and Watt was surprised when the sheriff finally picked up the line with a curt, "Yeah."

"Sheriff. This is Watt Miller. I need some kind of information on this situation, this shooting over at the school last night."

Silence on the line for a moment. Watt continued.

"I'm certain you realize I have to write a story. Hell, everybody in town's talking about it."

"Well, interview them." Watt expected the receiver to slam down, then he heard: "All right, come on over. I'll be here for ten minutes, so get by here fast."

The receiver shot down with a clunk.

Watt walked over to the courthouse, two blocks from The Herald's office. When Watt entered the front door -- next to the sign in relief letters proclaiming, "Remodeled 1871" -- and walked into the office, he didn't see the sheriff.

"Sheriff around?" Watt asked one of the deputies, a smart aleck chewing gum.

The deputy stared wide-eyed at the editor and smacked away on the gum. Saliva occasionally dripped out one corner of his mouth, but the deputy caught it quick, sucked it back in and swallowed.

"Mister editor," the deputy said mockingly.

Watt nodded, paying no attention and looking around the room.

"He's on the crapper. When you hear it flush next door, he'll be coming on back in here to talk to you."

Watt mumbled a "thank you" and walked out into the courthouse hall. He had tried hard to overcome his tendency to look down on lower-class people like the deputy, and he had managed during his life to get along well with the poor blacks and whites with whom he had come in contact. But people like the deputy were trash, and Watt despised having any dealings with them. Eventually Watt heard the gush of a toilet flushing. A door off to the side of the hall banged open and Sheriff Johnson emerged, tucking in his shirttail.

"Too long a day, my friend. Come on in," the sheriff said in a cordial way that surprised Watt. The two walked past the smacking deputy without a word to him and went into the sheriff's glass cage of an office in the back of the large open room. The sheriff closed the door and leaned against his desk, crossing his arms and nodding for Watt to take a seat in the crowded corner of the small office. Watt sat down and brought out the small notebook. The sheriff said nothing, but seemed to be waiting for the session to begin -- and end.

"I wonder if, first, you could tell me about the shooting death in as much detail as you can allow," Watt said. The sheriff kept his eyes on Watt as he listened, then ponderously moved his eyes and his head toward the ceiling. He thought before answering.

"What we got here, simple enough, is a professional-type murder. And what I mean by that is, well, it isn't the type of shooting we usually get here in the small towns."

This comment struck Watt as funny, although he didn't laugh. It sounded as if the sheriff just didn't put in an order for this type of crime very often and that's why this "type of shooting" hadn't occurred in Riverton.

"So, it's usually a big-city crime," the sheriff said. "In addition to it being odd, real unusual for us, it was planned. That's what I mean by 'professional.'"

Now Watt felt confused. The sheriff could see this.

"So as not to sound too round-about, this is an execution-type killing. Now, we don't think some dark-suited mobster came through here last night, opened up the school, forced Basford to the second floor, shot him to death, then headed back to Miami or Atlanta. What I mean to say, confidentially, is that the perpetrator probably is still around here or is here often enough to know his way around."

The sheriff eased back slightly on the desk, hung a leg over the corner and rocked his foot back and forth. Watt nodded and wrote several lines in the notebook. He seemed to understand.

"So we have a serious crime figure in and around the county?" Watt asked, still jotting notes.

"We don't know that. What we think is this. But I don't want you quoting me on it, and I don't want you printin' it either. The shooting was well planned out and carried off without a hitch far as we can see and with few clues for us. I say without a hitch, and by that I mean we think the killer believes that. But he's got one problem, and I can't talk any more other than to fill you in on some details. I'm tellin' you this because I need your help and I don't think I'm going to get any from that snoopy bastard who writes for the Valdosta daily."

"Whatever I can do, Sheriff, but I do need to run some kind of story," Watt looked up at the officer, pen and notebook poised for more.

"Well, you got to promise me not to run this. Yet, anyway. Maybe next week. OK?"

"Sure. I'll cooperate if you give me more details than you give the dailies."

"All right, just this. There was a witness. That was the killer's mistake, or rather his misfortune. Now, you keep that in confidence -- or I'll kick your pink butt all the way to Sunday."

With that, Sheriff Carroll Johnson gave an ashen-faced Watson Jennings Miller IV the details of Louis Basford's death, blood, guts and all.

Watt had a reasonable story for the next week's edition. What had seemed such a bother earlier that afternoon, came into place fairly well. He bent over his desk and picked up the second sheets on which he had written a first draft. He had never learned to type, and writing his stories out in longhand drew jokes and complaints from the paper's typesetters. He scrawled legibly enough, but at every turn

one of the young women compositors would badger him
about any word or sentence they couldn't read. He wrote the
story straight and in his usual style, which he had learned by
reading wire stories and other news accounts in the Atlanta
newspapers.

A Riverton man was shot to death at the old
Graystone High School Wednesday a week ago. Sheriff
Carroll Johnson identified the victim as Louis Basford,
who worked at a local pool parlor.

The shooting rocked the town last week, and
residents expressed concern for their safety.

"That just doesn't happen around here," City
Commission Chairman Wiley Dukes said. "We've had
our share of drug problems, but murder like this one has
never before resulted from that."

The commissioner quickly clarified that he was not
suggesting the shooting death was in any way connected
to a drug deal. "That happens all the time in big places
like Macon and Atlanta, but not here," he said.

Sheriff Johnson refused to comment on what might
have motivated the shooting death, but he agreed with
the commissioner on one point.

"What we got here is a big-city type murder," the
sheriff told the Herald. "It isn't the type of shooting we
usually get here in the small towns."

Mr. Basford was found alive but unconscious early
Thursday morning. He was taken to the Riverton
Hospital where he died. Dr. Simpson Millgrove of the
hospital medical staff performed a post-mortem
examination.

Mr. Basford died from bullet wounds to his chest
and stomach, the doctor said.

The sheriff said the shooting occurred on the second
floor at the top of the stairway in the northeast corner of
the building. He said Mr. Basford fell and rolled down
the steps and was found on the landing near the front

door.

Asked if Mr. Basford could have walked part of the way down the stairs, the sheriff replied, "No comment."

Mr. Basford was employed as a bartender at the pool hall located on South Barnes Street in Riverton.

Louis Basford left no known survivors. He is preceded in death by his mother, who passed away last April. His father, William K. Basford, a retired mill worker, died several years ago.

With that Watt had gone as far as he could go with the story. He knew there must be more going on with the case, especially since the sheriff had a witness. Still, he was writing for a weekly newspaper, and something could turn up over the weekend. The sheriff might call him and tell him more. Maybe they would make an arrest. If he thought about it, he may be able to figure out the witness's identity. Perhaps Brooks Sheffield, who seemed to have disappeared, would give him a clue. Ever the dreamer, Watson Jennings Miller IV floated on. Then he sank on the notion that none of these things would happen.

On his drive home out North Houston Avenue, Watt became increasingly dejected. Then he saw the blue, again parked in front of a large house just north of the courthouse. Lights were on in the house's front rooms at ten-thirty on a street that usually went dark earlier. He wheeled the truck across one of the street's turnarounds and headed back by the house, driving slowly, easing past the Volvo and another car parked behind it.

So Brooks Sheffield had returned and was probably inside the house right now. But Sheffield could wait. Watt had his story, the basic facts at least, for next week's edition. If something turned up, fine. If not, he had his story. He was, after all, very late for dinner, and he knew Jenny would be upset about this most unusual break in their routine. Watt shifted into low and turned the truck toward home. On the way, he put together what he was certain would make a reasonable apology both to Jenny and her parents.

Chapter 8 - Gabriel

Coffee in Sara's old kitchen smelled delightful, and Brooks particularly enjoyed the aroma this morning. His dark mood had lifted in the two weeks since the shooting. Sara soothed him. He had spent most of the past week with her, going to the school a few times to pick up clothes and check the mail. Brooks felt good. He appreciated Sara, and he was growing fond of her house. The coffee made, its smell blended with the essences of two generations of oil cloth on the table, saturated with herbs, spices, the fumes from the gas range and spills from bottles of vinegar, cooking sherry and sipping whiskey, which, over the years, in both the preparation of food and the celebration of momentous events, had sustained the Compton family's life.

Brooks was preparing breakfast this Thursday morning while Sara got dressed upstairs. Brooks took his turn making the coffee and setting out the light breakfast of granola, apple juice, coffee and toast.

In front of him on Sara's kitchen table was The Riverton Herald. On the front page, a second story about Louie Basford's death was featured prominently, although this shorter account provided nothing new about the murder.

This did not surprise Brooks. After his father's death and after Brooks sold the paper, journalism in Riverton had softened. Informative reporting had vanished, save stories like this about Louie Basford or coverage of the school board and city commission; these articles did provide a few bare facts. Mostly the newspaper's coverage ran shallow and reported only the veneer of community life: Births, deaths, marriages, social occasions illustrated with multiple pictures of each event. The Riverton Herald had lost its bite and had deteriorated into a mere toothy grin of a newspaper, filled with life's innocuous moments, packed with things important only to a small social elite. Goodness ruled the paper's columns, glibness wrote the words, and a positive attitude held a tight editorial hand on stories about the bright outlook for Riverton's future. The Chamber of Commerce's development efforts, well intended but fruitless as they were, carried greater weight in the Herald's pages than insights into the reasons for Piscola County's economic lassitude or follow-ups to the arrests of crack cocaine dealers the year before. The paper failed in its perspective and understanding of the community. These simply did not exist in the Herald, now a voice that never spoke. For seventy-eight years, Brooks' father and grandfather had fashioned that voice and with it announced and enunciated the events and dramas, good and bad, that affected Riverton and the county. Brooks blamed himself for selling the newspaper into silence.

Six months ago, law officers raided and arrested twelve crack dealers in Riverton's poor neighborhoods. The Herald ran one story with a banner headline, reporting the facts adequately. The next week's edition aggravated Brooks when the paper neglected to follow up on the drug raid. The newspaper ignored reporting the reasons behind the drug problem that had spread throughout the small community and about the families touched by this terrible, criminal affliction. What was worse, the paper by its silence seemed to lend support to thinking that the crack arrests had ended the town's drug problem.

Brooks gazed out the window. A young girl walked past. He had seen her many times at her house near the school, but until now had not realized she was pregnant. She was, he realized, the girl he'd seen last summer, just after he moved into the schoolhouse. He had seen her talking to an older man, then getting in his car and driving off with him. He watched her now as she walked up Houston Avenue toward the courthouse. Where was that man now? These thoughts discouraged him. Still, these were surmountable thoughts, and he valued Sara too much to allow himself to backslide into the murky feelings stirred by the shooting. He let the newspaper, drugs and awful social injustice against Riverton's poor people slip away.

He turned his thoughts to toast for Sara, a woman he cared for increasingly and liked doing little things for. The toaster pinged, almost on cue. Sara came into the room, Brooks pointed out the Basford follow-up story. Then they sat down to breakfast, ignoring the subject of the shooting and talking about other things. Talking playfully, as would two people in love.

"Well if you like it, I'll try it," Sara said, picking up the quart jar of apple juice and reading the label before trying this new dish. Her promise was bold, but she hesitated on the notion that granola soaked in apple juice, instead of milk, was palatable breakfast food. Love, she thought, makes you do strange things.

"It's good for you. Think of it that way," Brooks said, trying to dissuade Sara's reluctance.

She studied the label.

"How do you know this stuff doesn't have that strange chemical in it?"

"Alar? I don't know. Hell, you bought it."

Giving up, she spooned granola into her bowl and added a small amount of juice.

"You need more than that," Brooks said. "I kinda drink it as I eat the granola."

"Look here. I'm trying this stuff because of my affection for you, not because I think its worthy of any serious attention. So let me eat it the way I want to eat it."

"OK. OK. But hurry up or you'll miss the school bus, little girl."

With that Sara got up from the table, walked over to Brooks and muscled an arm around his neck. Then she leaned over and planted her lips firmly on his right ear, moving her tongue in, out and around it. Brooks held tight and enjoyed this interruption for a moment before grabbing Sara's behind and pinching hard with all his fingers.

"No fair. You cheated," she said, rubbing her rear and retreating to her chair.

"How you figure that?"

"The rules are: No grabbing the love handles unless I'm totally out of control with passion and otherwise don't notice what you're doing."

"That's a new rule on me."

"Well, I understood you to know. The only time you ever grab me there is when I don't seem to notice. Until just then."

"Are there any other rules I don't know about?"

Sara chomped on a spoonful of granola. The tussle had gotten her excited.

"Mmm. Not too bad. There are numerous rules than lovers of some experience just know."

"And how do I rate in that arena."

Sara thought a minute, wrinkling both her nose and brow and looking up to the ceiling in pensive mimicry.

"I could give you the test, but it'll take a few hours."

"I'm all for it, I think."

"You have to take it at the beach or the mountains, the setting's important."

"Ahh."

"And since the setting's so important, you have to set aside the time to get there. The atmosphere has to be just right, too, preferably a cottage on a remote beach or a cabin on an isolated cliff. Ambience is everything. Also, the correct attire is desired, though not mandatory."

Brooks grinned at this. "Anything else for the exam?"

Sara got up and sidled against him, gently suggesting he slip his chair out so she could sit down on his lap.

"There are some other important ingredients... You..." She kissed him. "Me..." She kissed him again. "And a king-sized bed." She melted into his face.

They were halfway up the stairs, their arms entwined around each other, when the phone rang.

"Let it go," Sara blew into Brooks' ear.

He stopped and thought.

"Better get it. Could be the sheriff or Dub."

"Oh, you -- you flunk!" she called out as Brooks headed back down the stairs to the phone. "And your healthy hippie cereal sucks!" Still, she followed him toward the phone.

"Yeah," Brooks said. "Dubowski. What's new, anything?"

Brooks nodded at whatever Dub was saying. Sara stood near, arms folded.

"Sure. I'll be there."

Dub went on.

"Saturday night? I'll ask. He turned to Sara. "We... rather, you doing anything Saturday night? Dub wants to go jukin' again, maybe out to eat in Valdosta?"

"He asking you or both of us?"

Brooks held a hand over the receiver.

"Look. He wants you to come because he likes you. Of course he's asking both of us."

"Sure. Let's do it."

He told Dub fine and said goodbye. Sara looked at him.

"Seven o'clock OK?"

"Yes."

"I'm meeting him for lunch. He wants to talk about something."

"Anything on the shooting?"

"Probably. He wasn't giving details on the phone."

"When does he eat lunch? Not much before noon, I trust?"

"I'm meeting him at one."

"That won't be enough time."

"For what?"

"Your examination."

Brooks stepped to Sara and pulled her to him. "It will give me plenty of time for what I have in mind, college entrance exams aside, Professor."

"Slay me with passion," Sara said, allowing his lips to fold around hers and his tongue to slip into her mouth.

They tripped up the stairs, undeterred by the telephone, which rang again, and hurtled themselves onto the bed so fast they bounced. "Your cereal was really pretty good," she told him later. "Breakfast of Champions?"

Brooks arrived at Hamburger Heaven, on Lauren Street south of the school, at twelve forty-five. Farmers and store workers filled the few tables, and two lines formed, mostly for takeouts. He waited for a table and in a few minutes sat down at one. Dub arrived several minutes after one o'clock.

"I'm buying, so don't even get up. We'll lose the table," Dub said. The crowd began to thin and two other tables became available. Brooks kept his seat, telling Dub he would have a cheeseburger, French fries and a chocolate shake.

"Be right back," Dub promised.

That Dub seemed businesslike today did not deter his action on his first of two hamburgers, a large Coke and two orders of fries. He set down their paper trays of food and immediately examined the ketchup bottle. Not nearly enough. So Dub walked back to the counter for another bottle. This he brought back, tossing from one hand to the other and noticing it was only a third full. He sat down.

"How's the mustard supply? Oh well, don't matter. I don't eat the stuff and if you want any, you can fetch it."

Brooks examined the plastic mustard container without touching it. "Looks fine, I guess," he said, picking up a fry and eating it.

"You know I quit eating mustard after Georgia," Dub offered. "The reason then was that mustard was OK but somehow it just changed when I wasn't in easy reach of the Varsity. You know, those onion rings and fries turned yeller mustard to ambrosia. Then in the seventies, they started making it brown instead of yeller. Pansy French mustard, I guess. Tastes worse than sour mule shit smells and looks about the same."

Brooks laughed at this loquaciousness, which was, after all, Dub Campbell's trademark, his brand. He turned a phrase or regaled in a tale about anything whether mundane or extraordinary. Dub attacked the burger with first his mouth agape, then by closing lips fully around nearly half the bun, double layer of beef, cheese, lettuce, tomato and oozing mayonnaise and ketchup. On first chomp he took off a good third of the hamburger. A ketchup man above all else, he contemplated the burger as he chewed the first portion and analyzed its flavor. Not enough ketchup, so he applied an ample coating across the line of his initial attack. Then he covered his own two orders of fries in ketchup. But this time he was ready for another crunch on the bun and its ingredients, a lot of which dripped onto the paper plate.

"Ah, nurse," Brooks motioned to a waitress behind the counter. "A case of ketchup, please." She looked confused, but brought out another bottle to Brooks, this one filled to the top. She glanced at Dub Campbell's jaw movement and darted back to her post behind the counter.

Brooks took his own meal slow and easy. Once Dub consumed his first burger, he slowed down a bit on the rest of the meal, but in no time he was munching on his last fry. Then he started talking. He told Brooks the case was going nowhere. He said the sheriff speculated on several people who could have shot Louie. The sheriff thought someone ordered the killing while someone else pulled the trigger. Who, Brooks asked, masterminded the killing? Dub said he couldn't say whom, but the sheriff had several people in mind.

"I don't understand," Brooks said. "This certainly sounds like big-crime stuff."

"It is, in Riverton. The drug trade has matured since you were an editor down at the Jacksonville paper. Used to be, people just used this area for drug drops, hauling the bulk of stuff off to sell in the cities and cutting out some for college campuses here and there. Now days, this is a sizeable drug market in itself, mainly crack, but also plenty of others including the perennial favorite for your hippie friends, marijuana. There ain't a safe haven from drugs anymore,

Brooks. It's everywhere, big towns and small, all across America. And it's killing this part of the country."

"So you all are saying this was drug-related?"

"Could be, though not a deal, according to what you overheard. Sheriff doesn't think Louie Basford was smart enough to tie his shoes, let alone work in the drug trade. He was dumber than a day-old turd. Didn't have one dab of sense. On the other hand, the sheriff reasons that Louie in fact may have gotten involved with drugs and got in over his head. That, or gambling. Seems that, according to the regulars, Louie's been spending less time in the pool room lately."

"Who's he work for?"

"That's what I want to show you. Let's get out of here and take a ride."

They rode in Dub's state-issued car. On the way Dub answered Brooks' question.

"Louie worked for a man named Sam Warren. He owns a bunch of pool halls, but the sheriff isn't convinced Sam did it."

"Why not?" Brooks asked.

"This man has a bunch of people working for him, and while he pretty much runs things himself, Louie was way down on the totem pole with him. Could be him. Sheriff thinks that might be just a little bit too obvious. You know how it is."

Dub thought for a moment, squinting into the road ahead. "Any way you look at it, Sam is pretty clean. Runs an honest business and keeps out of trouble. Doesn't tolerate any drug mischief in or around his pool halls, obeys the liquor laws, and operates, at least in most folks' view, above suspicion, so the sheriff thinks."

"What do you think?" Brooks said.

"Sheriff and I disagree totally. He swears I'm wrong, and quite frankly I don't have anything to go on, so he may be right. Except for one thing."

"That being?"

"Just what you said. Louie called his killer Boss, and nicknames aside, meaning possibly as I Work For You. And I don't think the sheriff is giving that reasoning a fair hearing."

They drove south of Riverton and crossed the Florida line.

Brooks knew where they were headed, to baseball cap city, the Starlite Lounge.

A surprising number of people were in the bar for early afternoon. "Shift at the paper mill just changed," Dub explained.

Brooks noticed the same bartender was on duty, and he recognized one of the local rednecks, a man shooting pool, who had been in the place when they were there before. Several groups of people crowded around tables, drank beer and whiskey, and smoked cigarettes. Dub and Brooks found a small corner table, and as they sat down Brooks' eyes again drifted to the baseball caps. Dub went to the bar and ordered a beer for Brooks and a Coke for himself.

In the laughter, behind the music, through the smoke and across the room in the back, a figure emerged. An old man had walked into the pool hall and moved about at the far end of the bar as if he owned the place. He talked with the bartender before ducking into a door, probably to an office. When the old man came out he had a case of liquor. He moved it midway behind the bar, bent down out of sight and when he walked away he held an empty box and set it down, closing the door and locking it. He said a few more things to the bartender before taking a stool. The bartender brought the old man what looked like a glass of ice water. The man, paying no attention to the refreshment, wrote in a small notebook he had pulled from his coat pocket. Dub noticed the old man, too, and excused himself for a trip to the men's room. Brooks watched as Dub stopped and said hello to the old man, then proceeded to the restroom.

Shortly after Dub disappeared, the lounge's front door opened and two guys walked in. One saw the old man and went back to talk with him. Brooks could barely hear the conversation, the voices muddled in the echo of the building, the music and the racket in the poolroom, but he could tell by their expressions it was congenial.

"Sam, how are you?" one of the men said.

"Well, hey there, Newton. I'm fine, fine. Just got back from a fishin' trip in Florida. How's this ugly lookin' bastard with you?"

"Fair, Mr. Sam. Fair." The other man grinned and nodded.

Then the conversation settled down into quiet tones Brooks couldn't make out. The old man escorted the two men out the back door and had not come back in when Dub returned.

"You see the man at the end of the bar?"

"Yes. Looked familiar."

"That's Sam Warren."

"Seems pretty harmless to me."

"Now you know better than that, mister ex-newspaper editor. You are drooling your fair-haired innocence all over the place. Let's go."

They left the Coke and beer practically untouched on the table.

Watt Miller got to the office early. For the first half-hour or more, he passed time reading the Atlanta and Jacksonville papers -- rather, he was skimming the papers. He downed a cup of coffee and ate a bran muffin.

A minute, several minutes, went by. He checked his watch. Several minutes more. He looked at the vintage Regulator ticking over the desk. Time about the same, not much had passed. A minute, several minutes, half an hour, then an hour slowly went by. Time crawled.

By ten-thirty on Friday morning, Watson Jennings Miller IV sat at his desk passing time, agonizing over his life and, once again, putting off definitive action on the story at hand: Louie Basford's murder.

OK, OK. I tried the aggressive reporting route and where did it get me? Nowhere. So now what to do?

He threw the loose stack of papers into their dumping corner.

Mrs. Pinson brought the mail in and piled it in a wire basket on the counter.

Watt got up, went to the counter, and brought the basket to his desk. A new Editor & Publisher magazine, which he never read, flew across the small office, landing on top of the newspapers in the corner. The basket held several neighboring weeklies, all rolled in white or pink or green mailing wrappers. To pass the time, the crawling time, Watt thumbed through pages of each paper. Then, with a pewter-handle letter opener, he sliced the edges of a dozen envelopes and after cursory reading tossed the contents of each into another wire basket, this one a permanent fixture on the desk. Finally, he set upon the weekly package from the state press association: Memoranda, a monthly newsletter and several small national ads to run in the Herald.

End of the pile.

The day still had five or six hours of obligatory office time.

What could Watt do?

For the next hour and a half, he turned his attention to social columns, death notices, wedding announcements and community calendar items dropped overnight in the front door's copy slot. After editing slowly and carefully, calling the funeral home to confirm the time of one funeral, marking and writing headline instructions, he carried these to the typesetter in the back shop.

He left for a solo lunch just after noon.

By one-fifteen, Watt was back in the office at his desk, pulling and tugging at himself now to do something about the big story. He checked with Mrs. Pinson about some ads that were not yet in. He picked up some type from the typesetter, proofed it and sent the corrections to the back.

At two o'clock, perhaps more out of boredom than duty

and along with a need to move around, Watt mustered the
gumption to do something. He picked up a notebook and
headed out the door with his jacket. His day would pass
much quicker now.

He started the pickup and repeated his visit of a week
ago to the school.

"You looking for the Schoolhouse Man, mister?"

Watt jumped when he heard the voice, no more than
three feet from him. He turned around to see an older man
standing there, leaning toward him real close. What struck
Watt about the man, who must have been fifty-five to sixty
years old, was the one gnarled, skinny rod of a gold tooth
protruding from a purple upper gum. His large bottom lip
rolled inward, hidden by the overhang of his upper lip, and
his yellow, bloodshot eyes bugged out at Watt. His sour
breath and his filthy clothes, all of him, smelled like a rancid,
near-empty bottle of dirt-cheap liquor. The man exhaled
heavily, his lips twisting into a half-grin, a grisly expression
Watt found unsettling.

"Err... yes. Brooks Sheffield's who I'm after," Watt
replied. "You happen to know where he is?"

The old man stared at Watt a moment.

"He don't seem to be 'round here much after that
shootin'. Ain't seen him since yes'day."

Without thinking about it, Watt turned into a reporter.
"What do you know about that shooting last week?"

"The man's dead, and I reckon he's done buried."

"Yes, well, I know that. But what I mean to say is, did
you see anything?"

"Who you, mister?"

Watt explained who he was and that he was looking for
information on the dead man.

The old man smiled, but without answering, he stared
right into Watson Jennings Miller IV, as if he saw this
scrubbed young man's emptiness, his disjointed career path,
his shabby life charades. He considered the young fool he

saw and laid forth his ground rules, which for him came
pretty easily.

"I ain't talking to no sheriff, mister. If you get any ideas
about that, don't ask me to."

"I don't understand. Why wouldn't you?"

"Why don't matter none, mister newspaper man. Just be
knowin' I ain't talkin' to the sheriff. You writin' a story, ain't
you?"

"Yes. Tell me, what do you know about all this?"

"You gimme twenty dollars and a ride?"

Watson Jennings Miller IV took no time to contemplate
this opportunity. He reached into his pocket for some bills,
counted several out and placed them in the older man's hand.
Then they both got into the truck. They rode. And they
talked. Time passed with the scent of cow manure and pig
muck, dried cut cornfields and the white hints of picked
cotton fields that speckled Piscola County. They stopped at a
liquor store in Valdosta, where the old man spent his twenty
dollars on whiskey and came back out to the truck to squeeze
Watt for more money for beer.

The old man told a good story. Almost too good. So
good it scared Watt to death. His reporting venture had been
fruitful, but what in the world would he do with the
information?

Finally, at ten that night, he dropped the old man off on a
back neighborhood road two blocks from the school and
headed home to Jenny. Glad to see him, she offered no
protest about his absence, though the recent late work hours
still disappointed her.

Watt rarely came into the office on Saturday, and if he
did he usually left by noon. Today, however, he had stayed
through the afternoon, having come back in after lunch. The
cleaning woman was sweeping up when he arrived. Soon she
had emptied all the trashcans and mopped the entire office
floor, carefully and quickly moving the mop around his feet.
After collecting her pay envelope, she disappeared, leaving

the pungent, piney odor of cleaning fluid and the office to Watt.

The magnitude of this story perplexed, even frightened Watt, and he was unsure how to handle it. The man was Gabriel Wheeler. Watt had not known the man, but had heard of him. Some people called him "Corndog." Watt hadn't asked the man where he picked up the nickname. The whole time Watt called him "Mr. Wheeler." Gabriel seemed to enjoy the formality, but later explained the nickname.

Gabriel Wheeler had worked many years at the school as its janitor, and that's where he earned his sobriquet. School cohorts coined the name easily enough from Gabriel Wheeler's affection with this cheap dish served so often in the school cafeteria. On days corndogs were served, Gabriel willingly took the leftovers to his room for snacks. Now he lived nearby and over the years still had kept an eye on the comings and goings at the school. Mostly it was school maintenance people stopping by for supplies they stored there, but occasionally lovers had sought out the abandoned building's oak trees as night harbor for their parked cars.

Then, Brooks Sheffield moved into the building. Wheeler said Sheffield caused little change at the school, from what he could see. People still parked under the oaks, and no one other than people in the neighborhood really knew or cared that someone lived in the school.

"They kept on drivin' their cars up under those old oak trees in the back, gettin' their business done and drivin' off again," Wheeler said. "I saw cars and trucks back there every week. Not a crowd, you know, just one car a time. People gettin' their business."

From Watt had gathered from Mr. Wheeler, whoever killed Louie Basford had planned it deliberately and may have figured the body wouldn't be found for some time, not knowing the school was occupied. Louis Basford was shot on the top floor of the building and had fallen or stumbled almost to the basement before keeling over the last time. Mr. Wheeler described the blood he had seen in puddles on the floor and splotches on the walls and winding up the stairway from the landing on the basement entrance. And Louie's killer probably lived in Riverton. Probably someone Louie knew, Gabriel said.

Gabriel Wheeler swore he didn't recognize the man who walked out of the building after the shooting, got into a pickup truck and drove away. Corndog felt certain, however, that Brooks Sheffield did not drive the truck. Watt had a lot of questions, many unanswered by Gabriel with sometimes emphatic but more often casual denials. He could not use Gabriel Wheeler's comments as a basis for a news story, since the sheriff would want to know the source. Without answers from an official source, such as the sheriff or his own witness, Watt really didn't have a story. Gabriel conditioned the interview on Watt's agreement not to make him talk to the sheriff, and telling the sheriff about Gabriel would break that promise. But Gabriel knew more than he told, Watt knew that, and Gabriel probably knew who killed Louie, too.

After getting home so late on Friday, Watt knew, Jenny would either become accustomed to waiting -- or divorce him. He doubted the latter, not with a baby coming. Now, here he was, working all Saturday afternoon. It was unheard of, to Jenny, maybe a rival she'd never perceived. Amends could be made.

He ran everything over in his mind again. During the drive back from Valdosta and as the old man sank deeper into drunkenness, Watt had time to plan how he would handle the story. That thinking and the last two hours of this Saturday afternoon led him to a decision. He couldn't tell the sheriff, but he could tell someone -- at least, he could let someone know what was going on. Now Watt, in the manner that often eluded him, turned to decisive action. From his position as newspaper editor, the decision was cowardly and inappropriate, but as Watson Jennings Miller IV, his idea was brilliant, a real jewel. Ready now to bail out, first he had to deliver a message, a private news story between him and someone else.

Watt leaned over his desk with a stack of second sheets before him and began to write.

Sam Warren's satisfaction with himself soared this evening. That afternoon, right under the nose of the Georgia Bureau of Investigation, he had arranged with two Georgia boys to provide escort services for their club's convention in Orlando next month. Charlotte already had started making the arrangements. She and Sam both had just made a shiny nickel up front on the deal, and Sam felt good.

So why did he also hold deep down a sense of uneasiness? He wondered about this. More than two weeks had passed since he shot and killed Louie Basford. He himself had recuperated -- while establishing a pretty solid alibi on the night of the shooting -- and was ready to get back to his routine. Tonight, though, the uneasiness crept in on him in a giant wave, which rose slowly and far away but nevertheless built to a force. He would have to do something about this. Sam sat in his Cadillac and turned on the ignition key to start up the engine. A light indicated the car's electronic balancing mechanism was preparing a ride of ease and comfort. Sam wheeled out of the Starlite's dirt-and-gravel parking lot and headed toward his farm.

He delighted in having Gracey over that night. She came to spend a few days with Uncle Sam. Gracey wasn't a regular employee at Charlotte's Web. She usually worked the trade in Valdosta and Tallahassee by phone from an escort listing. Slender and scarred, her manner disputed her name. Both Sam and Charlotte felt certain she had worked as a street hooker at one time. She was popular turning tricks, but she was unpredictable. Charlotte kept her around for conventions and other jobs, but never allowed her near the upscale customers who usually frequented the Web. To Sam, Gracey was his kind of whore: Slinky like a cat, kinky like a Mexican donkey and trashy, the way Sam liked them. He invited Gracey over after telling Charlotte the little bleached blonde belonged on a farm because Gracey sounded like the name of a good milk cow. "And the milk she gives, I could drink all day," Sam had said.

He pulled up to his back door and walked inside. The lights were off. He walked into the kitchen and saw Gracey on the table.

"What in the hell are you doing, girl?" Sam said, after flipping on the light.

Like a trashy cat, ready for a big tom, Gracey sat on the kitchen table, Indian fashion. She didn't have to answer. Her smile told all.

As Sam went to the table, his uneasiness ebbed. He would get back to thinking up a plan tomorrow. Maybe Gracey could help him just as she was beginning to help him right now, touching his arm and pulling him close.

Chapter 9 - The Chase

Brooks' longing to talk with Harriet in Atlanta had diminished over the last four or five days. Perhaps that was the reason he called her now. He refused to lose contact with her, and he knew Harriet, emotionally solid and independent as she was, would not call him unless she had heard about his situation.

His first try, on Saturday morning, had reached a solemn, recorded version of Harriet's voice on her answering machine. That had pressed his determination, and now, just before noon, he dialed the number again, dropping four quarters at the operator's urging, into the pay phone in the parking lot of the Hamburger Heaven.

He heard Harriet's blunt way of answering the phone. "Yes."

"Hi, it's Brooks."

"Really? Where have you been the last month or so?"

"Right here in the river city."

"Well, I wish I could say Atlanta misses you, but it doesn't. Life goes on."

Brooks wanted to ask Harriet whether she missed him, whether she cried one tear after he left. He suppressed the urge and let this thought drift away.

"This must be a special occasion. Your calling."

"Yes. Couple of things. First, hadn't talked with you in awhile, and second, things are rocking along here at a brisk pace, euphemistically."

"They are, huh?"   Harriet never would ask for an explanation.

"Well, things are sticky. You know, I told you I'm living in the old high school."

At this, as she had done earlier every time Brooks had

mentioned the school to her, Harriet burst into laughter.

"Well, I still don't believe it. That's too decisive for you, Brooks. But, go ahead." Her giggles subsided, but the delight in her voice remained.

"Well, a couple of weeks ago, a guy was shot dead in the school."

"What?" Harriet's voice lost its luster.

"Yes. A local guy. Police think he may have been involved in some kind of underhanded activity. Drugs, something like that."

"Brooks, are you OK?"

"Yes, sure. I'm fine."

"Thank God," she responded, accent expressing some relief and hiding her inner disbelief, her doubt and uncertainty and her concern for a man she loved.

"I was scared to death. And I haven't told anyone yet but you how scared."

"Well, are you OK staying in the building now? I mean, drug dealers around there or anything like that?"

"No, no. I'm OK there," Brooks said. "But I'm a witness."

"You're what?"

"Yeah. I heard the whole thing. Didn't see it, but I heard it."

"You aren't in jail, are you?"

"No, no. I'm a witness, not the killer." As Harriet paused, he thought, Miss Cool is trying to collect herself. "Well, why the hell didn't you call before now?"

"A long story. You know me. It's been tough."

"Hmm. I know how you react."

Another pause.

"Why didn't you call?"

Harriet tightened, bolstering herself for the unknown. "You're not staying at the school anymore, are you?"

"No."

"Who is she?"

"A friend. In fact, you know her or know who she is. But

don't let's get into that. That's not why I called."

"OK. Fine. You always have your needs, Brooks. Poor doggy. You know I love you to death. I never told you this before, and don't take this wrong, but you grew up in several ways and in others you remained a little boy."

Brooks responded with the patience he had learned in knowing Harriet over the years. He knew he had to listen, and that was the easiest thing to do right now. This was her time to vent, in her own way, her feelings about him. This was her way of saying, "Damn it, I love you."

"Yeah?" he said.

"Your problem is you love women. You worship women. You're not like a great many other men, Brooks. You don't use women and you actually treat them as equals. You're not above them and you feel no need to control them. You're without match, to my knowledge, and that's not necessarily a compliment. In a way it is, yes. I guess... You have to be mothered and smothered with affection. What you deserve is a big-hearted woman who can heal you emotionally and take you on physically. You need so much more than a lover and a shrink, damn it..."

Brooks listened to the muffled sniffling that followed and merely mumbled agreement as Harriet resumed her discourse.

"Whoever she is, I'm jealous," she said. "And that's all I'm saying about it. You know, I wondered why you never invited me down. This explains it."

"Sorry."

"No, you're not."

"Yes, I am. Really."

"Are you sure you're OK? Look, whoever this woman is, and I don't want to know, particularly if I know her, tell her she had damn well better care for you."

"I will."

"How's your gut?"

This phrase took Brooks back a few years, back to when Harriet's healing hand had touched and soothed him after

Jane's death. It was a loving question, meant, then, to break open and bring some light into a moment of deep sadness.

"Holding together reasonably."

"One other thing, and then I have to go."

"Yes?"

"Have you been to the beach lately?"

"Not since the last time with you."

"Good. Don't get any ideas. But remember, you owe me a beach trip. This time, I'll bring the books since there aren't any decent bookstores south of Macon. And leave Miss Big-Hearted home."

"OK. And Harriet?"

"What?"

"My feelings about you haven't changed in forty years. They never will."

"Thanks Brooks. Me, too. Bye."

"Goodbye."

He held the phone well after hearing the click from her end of the line. He just stood there, no emotion right then, smelling the grease in the air from Hamburger Heaven's grill.

He felt fine, and he wondered why.

"Where is Dub taking us this time?"

Sara flitted around the house like a schoolgirl. Before Brooks could answer, she had darted upstairs.

After spending the morning shopping, all afternoon she had washed clothes, sipped beer, done her hair, tried on various dresses, ironed at least two, and generally paid no attention to Brooks. Tonight promised a big event for Sara, since, apparently, no man had asked her out to dinner in months, maybe years, and, to her delight, two men would escort her tonight.

Brooks had paid a lot of attention to Sara lately, so much so she had to shoo him away to make time for her classes and doctoral research. In little over a week, Brooks had wrapped her in love, warmth and companionship, as Sara viewed it, but Brooks thought he had received more than she had from the relationship. He needed a woman and a friend like Sara, and he gratefully repaid her with attention, something she badly needed.

She bounded back down the stairs and into the kitchen, where Brooks stood opening a beer can.

"Well, where?"

"Suspect it's a place south of town on the river. Place called Shakespeare's."

"Is it that dinner theater?" She took a sip from her beer and set the can back on the table where she had left it earlier in the afternoon and probably would let it sit the rest of the day.

"No. Shakespeare's is a legend, of sorts."

"Oh, yeah. I've heard all kinds of stories about that place. Never been there, though. Are you sure it's safe for young, nubile women?" Sara wrapped her arms around Brooks and listened to his answer.

"It's safe... for you... with us." He kissed her on the forehead, and she kissed him back then broke her embrace for the beer.

"Shakespeare's is way out in the sticks south of Valdosta. Advertising guy from Atlanta opened it years ago. His name is Shakespeare Willaford, an honors graduate and former class president at Emory. Two years out of school, he got sick and tired of Atlanta and came back south, as I did. Only he came back sooner. He opened a fish restaurant, and thirty years later he and the establishment are legends."

"And his name? It's that advertising flash?"

"Shakespeare? No. Dempsey is Willaford's given name. Shakespeare is a nickname. I heard he was a real card in school. He would see a girl he wanted to take out and send her a note with a few lines from Romeo and Juliet. Most fell head over heels for it, so guys started calling him Shakespeare. Then they started hiring him to write their own love notes. You'll probably get to meet the Bard himself tonight."

"And is he still such a slick mover?"

"Oh, I guess he's a nice guy. Dub knows him pretty well."

"And the food?"

"The usual South Georgia restaurant fare. Steaks, fried fish, shrimp and an OK salad bar. And, plenty of bourbon."

"I guess I can endure," Sara said. "Present company excepted."

"You'll have all the company you can keep over there."

With that, Sara picked up the can of beer and skipped out of the kitchen. Brooks thought about following her, but right now he knew better.

At six-thirty, Brooks went to the door and through the bottom edge of translucent cut glass saw two big hands, each clutching large brown paper sacks. He opened the door for Dub Campbell.

Dub came in and headed for the kitchen, put the bags on the table, and took out a quart bottle of Beefeater gin and a pint of extra dry vermouth, and a fifth of Wild Turkey.

"Are you planning a celebration, or what?" Brooks asked.

"No, just a little cocktail before dining in Shakespeare's splendor," Dub replied, going to a cabinet for tumblers, then refrigerator for ice as if he had been making drinks in this house for years. Then he turned to Brooks.

"And looky here," he said, taking a bottle of Möet White Star champagne out of the other sack. "This is for the lady. Compliments of your escort for the evening."

Brooks beheld the bottle in wonder. "Sara's surprise?"

"Yep," said Dub, putting the bottle in the refrigerator. "Where is she, getting dressed?"

"All afternoon," Brooks said, emptying a beer can into the sink and eyeing the Turkey. The tumblers full of ice sat unattended. Brooks decided to let Dub do the honors since the gin was, after all, his treat.

Dub turned back to the larger of the brown bags and withdrew a large wedge of Brie wrapped in cellophane and a box of croissant crackers, along with a jar of large Spanish olives. All this amazed Brooks. No surprise about the liquor, but the champagne and cheese set him back.

"Where do you find this stuff down here?"

"The gettin' place. You Atlanta wimps don't have exclusive hold on upscale munchies and libations. You know that, boy?"

"Well, I guess they don't," Brooks said, raising his eyebrows and sighing at what promised to be a lively evening.

Dub found a large plate in another cabinet, then rifled several drawers for the right knife. He set the cheese on the plate and arranged the crackers.

"There. When your woman arrives for the evening, we'll be set to go."

"You're a real connoisseur, Dub Dee."

"That I am, my man."

Dub turned his attention to the gin and the glasses. He poured Brooks' glass half full, uncapped the vermouth and added a drop. Then he plopped in two olives. Brooks took it, held it to his lips, and sipped, ever so carefully. He then stirred the drink with a spoon. The silvery liquid swirled, mixing slowly as it frosted the glass. Dub prepared his martini and offered a toast.

"Between us boys -- to friendship. And the good work of Sheriff Johnson."

"Cheers to both," said Brooks. They sipped. "And what does the sheriff have to say about anything?"

"Nothing new."

"Hell, it's been almost two weeks."

"Hold your horses. These investigations take weeks, sometimes months, before an arrest is made. Best you can do is settle down and live life."

"That's fine. But there's only one little problem that has started eating on me today."

"And?"

"Well, this morning I called an old friend of mine in Atlanta. I don't think you ever met her. Harriet Browning?

She would have left years before you moved here. We grew up here in Riverton, went to school together and worked in Washington at the same time."

Dub nodded and listened.

"We're pretty close. Have been since Jane died."

"Dub raised his eyebrows, then looked upstairs."

"Yeah, well, there could be complications. But that isn't my worry."

"What is it then, if it ain't stirring up jealousies? What in hell could be worse?"

"Well, for one thing, whoever shot that guy could have figured out some things since the killing."

"For instance?"

"That I live in the schoolhouse. He may not have known and, after finding out, he could be wondering where I was that night. Was I there? Was I out? And if I was there, what could I have seen or heard? Most everybody in town knows that I live there, and a few people probably even think I'm a nut, or some sort of eccentric or somebody like that."

"No! You?" Dub said, cocking his head back. "Why would anyone think you would be a nut for living in an old, rundown schoolhouse?"

Brooks caught the sarcasm but let it pass. At least, he hoped it would pass.

"That why you been staying over here?"

"Why? Because I'm scared?"

Dub nodded. "Concerned is how I'd put it."

"I suppose, in a way, it may be. But I also happen to like Sara a lot."

"Figured that was the main reason."

"Look here. Am I in any danger?"

Dub looked up at the ceiling, returned his eyes to Brooks and sipped his drink.

"We've tossed that around. Don't think the sheriff is too concerned about anyone coming back and trying to keep you quiet. But we've discussed it. Likely they'll look for you around the school, assuming they know who you are. I think

if an all out hunt were on for you, we would have had some
hints by now. How scared are you, Brooks? And have you
seen or heard anything, like cars following you or strange
phone calls?"

"No. None of that."

"Well, you used to be a reporter, so you know the score
with the criminal element. Be careful, although I don't think
you have anything to worry about."

Brooks looked through the kitchen door and saw Sara's
feet on a stair step. She stood there, listening. When they
stopped talking, she proceeded down the steps.

Dub caught on to Brooks' attention to the stairs and he
said nothing.

Sara came into the kitchen wearing a strapless flower-
print dress, carrying a jacket on her arm. Her ample breasts
stood forth, cleavage displayed in an inviting way. She hid
her concern over the two men's conversation well, but her
breasts heaved in excited breathing. She smiled, walked up to
Dub Campbell and planted a wet, red-lipstick kiss on his left
cheek.

Dub nonchalantly set his martini on the kitchen counter.
He wiped his cheek, looked over at Brooks and said, "My
mama told me I'd turn to stone if a fast, loose woman ever
kissed me like that."

Sara leaned against the kitchen table by Brooks. She
didn't say a word. She just smiled.

"Cheese, madam?" Dub offered the plate to Sara.

She accepted, expressing her desire, too, for a drink.

Their Saturday night out with Dub Campbell was on its
way.

Well, for once, Watt's home on time, Jenny thought.
Never mind it was Saturday, which they usually spent
together. Never mind he hardly ever worked late even on
weeknights. Never mind his apologetic nature had waned in
light of all the above. But that was OK, she guessed. He was
home and that was important. She cooked dinner while Watt

relaxed in the pine-paneled den and watched "Hee Haw" on television.

Hee Haw? she thought, finding it curious since he never watched that show. That's strange. But never mind. He's home.

A dish bubbled in the oven, wild rice smothering six delicate quail her father had brought them on his last visit. Another twenty minutes and they would eat. She checked on the biscuits in the smaller oven, popping up fine with just a hint of golden browning on the top, and set about making the salad, sighing over the lack of radicchio in Riverton's grocery stores. Iceberg lettuce again, not even romaine this week.

Here I am, she thought, complaining to myself again. Must be the pregnancy. Still, Watt had seemed distant lately; they'd talked some, but it wasn't the shared intimacy they'd been accustomed to.

At dinner, Watt told her he would have to run an errand around midnight. He said he knew this was unusual, but it was part of the murder story. Jenny didn't take this well. She didn't understand his behavior of late, and this announcement confused her more than anything else. She left the table and went into the kitchen to cry. Watt knew this response, knew he had been neglecting her lately, so he gave her a few minutes before following to offer comfort. He held her as she sobbed into his shoulder. Then he told her.

"We're moving out of Riverton," he said. "I'm getting out of the newspaper business. Daddy will just have to understand. I think I'll go back to teaching. Maybe in Savannah."

At this, Jenny cried even more, but her tears flowed out of relief and joy rather than uncertainty. Watt could run any errand, any time, just as long as they could move back to Savannah soon! Nothing else mattered. Why he needed to go out at such an unusual hour, without explanation and without inviting her, was of no consequence now, for Jenny Willingham Miller of Savannah could go home. Her parents would make absolutely certain that her Savannah lifestyle, whatever her husband's income, would be on a par with theirs. Somehow, she knew, she, Watt and the baby would always be taken care of, no matter what Watt's next job adventure, his next pursuit, his next round of subsidized failure.

On a night in midwinter, drunk drivers often crowded the road winding through farms and woods and across the Piscola River. The road crosses its namesake and passes through a small farming community also named, like the road and the county, after the river, whose dark waters roll through and eventually pour into the more famous Suwannee River. Though paved, the road runs through backwoods, and on Friday and Saturday nights people who've had too much to drink take the otherwise less-traveled Piscola Road, crossing the river and passing through woods and fields on their way home to Riverton.

Over the years, careless driving and high speeds along the winding thoroughfare had caused tragic car wrecks that maimed and killed both the inebriated and the innocent alike.

On the Piscola County side of the river, about two hundred yards east of the bridge, stands a small granite obelisk -- a memorial to two people killed on the road in the 1930s. Located well off the road and in the woods, the monument sits out of sight of most motorists.

On a Saturday night, the Rev. Charles G. Stewart and his wife Emily were returning to Riverton from a Baptist ministers' conference in Statesboro. They were anxious to get home, having been away most of the week.

But while the Rev. Mr. Stewart would have prepared his Sunday sermons, conducted a funeral on Monday afternoon, and performed a wedding the next Saturday, he never had to fulfill any of those obligations. Around ten o'clock, he and his wife, two popular young leaders in the Riverton religious and civic community, died quickly and violently when a drunk driver swerved into the path of a lumber truck, causing the truck driver to turn sharply and crash head-on into the

Rev. Mr. Smith's Ford coupe. The accident threw Riverton into mourning for weeks.

In the late 1950s, a tragic one-car smashup killed the Graystone High quarterback and crippled another passenger for life. The quarterback had excelled in sports and academics, and his mourners put a bronze plaque on the wall next to the trophy cabinet near the principal's office. The trophy was gone but the plaque still read: "In memory of Jacob Grant Neely IV, Our Hero, Our Scholar, Our Inspiration, Who Died So Young. We Shall Remember Grant Always."

Nobody ever said Grant Neely was drinking the night of the accident. In fact, most people thought he should have been driving because he was probably the only sober one in the car.

The Piscola Road's hills and curves, the big oaks and pines on its shoulders, and the darkness of its deep dip and sharp curve at the river twisted bodies and steel into nothingness. There is no sense to this, adults of every era shake their heads and say. There is no sense to this at all, for the road has claimed too many over the years, and they need to straighten out the curve and get the drunks off the road. These solutions go unheeded, and the death rides continue year after year.

Several years after Grant Neely perished, his younger brother died along with another young man on this road. A third passenger was seriously injured, but survived. All had been drinking. The impact's force hurled Reston Neely's body from the car and into a bank of sand.

Sara knew all this, of course. She had grown up in Riverton and all her life had heard the stories about drunks weaving home on the Piscola Road. She had felt the tragedy, too, having known Reston Neely and the other two boys, but she couldn't think of this as she drove Brooks Sheffield's beat-up Volvo down the road. The thoughts never entered her mind. Right now, she just wanted to get herself and her soused companions in the back seat home safely.

Sara drove carefully. She just didn't dwell on the Piscola Road's reputation of death and destruction. That was fine until she was three miles outside Riverton. The courthouse clock would be tolling eleven.

By most measures, Dub and Brooks had behaved themselves during the evening and were calming down after singing their drunken hearts out early in the trip from Shakespeare's. Sara had taken control of the situation when they walked out of the restaurant, seeing that neither of the two men could drive home. She said she would drive, and Dub had acquiesced as long as he could sit up front with Sara.

"I mean, understand me, Sara," Dub had said. "I'm not trying to throw off Brooks and you, but I ain't gettin' in the back seat with someone of questionable tendencies, and if he's been driving Volvos all his life, he must be ... just that."

Brooks protested, and as they argued about it they both crawled into the back seat anyway. This was fine with Sara because she had isolated the party animals in their own little den. She could drive without Brooks easing his hand up her leg, which he had done several times on the way over to Shakespeare's, and without Dub honking his stories and songs loudly into her ear.

Right now they were settling down, so the trip back wasn't as bad as she expected when they first left the restaurant.

Then the glaring lights, brightened to blinding by fog lamps, rushed out of the darkness into her rear-view mirror. The car was probably a quarter-mile back but gaining steadily and weaving. When it didn't slow, Sara pushed the accelerator and looked for a side road, but there was nothing but cotton fields and, up ahead, some woods.

She responded quickly, methodically. As the car continued gaining, Sara planned her move. She surveyed the first field spreading out to her right. Big ditch. They would flip over for certain. On the left, a run of heavy woods between farms. The car's lights now brightened the inside of the Volvo, and the gap between her car and the pursuing vehicle closed to a few yards. Relief. She was relieved when, finally, the car slowed.

Sara held the steering wheel steady on the road and glanced sideways again for another out. On the left side of the road, woods opened up to another fenceless bare field. The lights wavered. The other car's weaving heightened the danger. Was the driver trying to pass or too drunk to hold it steady?

The too-bright reflection of headlights began to blind her. She could not see the road clearly. Her headlights helped little, showing no road or field clearance.

Dub and Brooks roused up, cursing and getting focused on what was happening.

All of a sudden, Dub seemed amazingly sober.

"Just hold her steady," he said. "That guy's been drinking."

"I know, Dub, that's why he won't back off."

"Tried slowing down?"

"No, just keeping a little ahead of him."

The car's horn blasted. Then the car swerved over to the left lane, but for some reason didn't try to pass.

"You all got your seat belts on?" Sara asked.

"I do. Why?" Brooks said.

"Hell no," cried Dub, fumbling for both ends of his belt, which was lost somewhere to the back and side of the seat.

"Hold on, then."

Sara eyed her window of escape up ahead, looking for a clear route.

The car behind straightened out of its weaving pattern and stayed directly on her. It moved up close, staying right on her bumper and backed off. What was going on? The hard thud answered that question for Sara. The car struck her bumper, thrusting the Volvo forward. A second bump rocked them even more, but a third caused less of an impact. Then the chase car backed off slightly.

Sara looked out across the fields, surveying telephone

poles and fences. The road shot out flat and straight ahead. She could aim the Volvo between two telephone poles and into the cotton field, which seemed to stretch forever across the road to their left. It was a clear shot and fairly level from the road to the field, although she expected the car to flip once it hit the field. She glanced into the mirror. The car slid left before cutting sharply back to the right.

"Here goes!" she yelled and hung onto the steering wheel as she turned it slowly but decisively to the left. Lights blinked, and the chase car's horn blared a steady protest as they catapulted off the shoulder.

The cotton field's rows slowed their bouncing progress as the Volvo bumped over clods and stubble. Sara held the steering wheel steady, kept her foot off the brake and let the car roll to a stop.

The other car vanished. No more lights. No more horn. The Volvo's engine idled, awaiting its driver's shift.

"Holy mother of Jesus! Everybody all right?" Dub said. Sara heard this, but nothing else. She collapsed in tears, her sobs blending with wails of panic and relief. They had ridden the Piscola Road's ride to near death and survived. Now, she remembered the road's horrible legacy, remembered it quite vividly, right up to the moment she saw state patrol car's flashing blue lights and was relieved help was on the way.

Brooks' head pounded as the wrecker chugged across the field to the Volvo. He held and comforted Sara and wrapped her shaking shoulders in his sport jacket. The air in the field felt cold, more the usual cold of the season than the evening's earlier balminess. Summer wasn't here yet, he thought, as he shivered and tried to stand without swaying. The effects of the martinis showed in his knees, and although he was clear-headed, he still felt shaky. Dub seemed in better shape, but then, Dub probably felt like this a lot, with his head in the vise-grip of a hangover and his belly in the gutter of pain and distortion from too much liquor consumed too quickly. Dub, Brooks thought, is a regular drunk. Guess that makes me... what? An occasional one?

A couple who had driven up after the accident and left to call the state patrol had returned and asked if they wanted a ride into Riverton. But the trio waited until the wrecker hauled the Volvo back onto the road. At the roadside, the wrecker eased the car down.

"Guess it might run," the wrecker driver said. He had been paid by Brooks upon arriving, so there was no need to go to the time and bother of towing this car into town if it would run, the man figured.

Brooks turned the key, and the motor started up fine. He was relieved, since he'd just spent a bundle on repairs.

"Sounds good," the wrecker driver said.

"Yeah, well, just don't drive off till we know we're rolling," Dub ordered.

The driver stood quietly, not saying a word. He recognized the GBI agent and wanted no trouble from him.

Sara got in the front seat, fastened her seatbelt, and asked Brooks if he were really able to drive. The state patrolman, walking to the car with Dub, looked at Brooks and suggested that perhaps it was better if the lady continued driving. Brooks complied, and Sara again slid behind the wheel.

She backed the Volvo up, and Brooks listened for any rattles and hoped the steering and other mechanisms had survived the rough ride across the field. Everything OK, they drove off with Dub waving a big thumbs up to the wrecker driver and the patrolman.

They arrived back at Sara's house at one-thirty. Without anyone insisting on it, Dub crashed on the sofa in Sara's living room. The kitchen can wait, Sara thought, and she didn't even bother going in to turn off the light.

Had she done so, she might have seen the rolled cone of yellow paper stuck into the open bottle of Beefeater gin. She might have noticed this strange sight and unrolled the pages to read the letter. But she didn't. The second sheets would have to wait until Sunday afternoon.

Chapter 10 - Missive

The handwriting was large and scrawling, the penmanship not unlike a child's:

To: Brooks Sheffield.

There are two witnesses to Louis Basford's murder. Sort of. One the sheriff knows about already. The other didn't really see the murder, but this person saw someone, and not you, walk out of the school and drive away within minutes after the person heard the shots. This witness lives close to the school. Cannot identify the person because promised not to.

This person described the truck as a late 1950s or early '60s Ford pickup, painted light blue or gray. Says it was hard to tell because of the darkness. Person has not seen the truck in years, but knows who used to own one like it and thinks still does. Truck had a rail and boards like the kind farmers used to haul hogs. But this rail was only one-sided, right behind the cab. The side rails and rear one -- forming a pen -- were missing.

These may be minor details, but they could help.

Whatever happens, you don't know me. You may know me, but don't acknowledge it. Please. And don't contact me.

I WILL NOT TELL WHO TOLD ME ALL THIS UNDER ANY CIRCUMSTANCES.

Some other things you may need to know. The person says he also saw the two people arrive at the school. They rode in together in the pickup. Says didn't even think about the arrival until much later after the shooting. But the person saw the pickup drive down the street north of the school and turn into the back lot.

Next day this person snooped around the school and saw the bloodstains and walked as far as the first floor of the stairway. Then person left building, apparently because person gets spooked or thinks someone might walk in.

How did I find this person? That's not important for you to know. Why am I doing this? Equally unimportant. But the reason is that you must want to have this case solved because you own the school. And I don't believe you had anything to do with this killing. Nor does the person mentioned here. Person says you ain't the nut everybody says you are. Person apparently knows you, though mentioned you don't know the person, or rather don't remember the person.

There's one other thing, Sheffield. Person says this probably is a simple thing because there are obvious connections. And this is why I suspect my person knows who did the killing: While vehemently denying person can identify the murderer, person does allow some suspicions about who did it. Several days after the shooting, person finally remembered who owned the truck he'd seen several years ago. Says it's plausible same man owns truck now. The 'funny link,' person says, is that the man who might have shot Basford spends a lot of time in Florida and has known Basford for many years. Person says Basford worked for the man who once owned the truck person remembers seeing several years ago.

You put two and two together from here. Person is right. This thing could be pretty simple and obvious. But remember, please, don't call or contact me -- ever!

Brooks put down the last of the seven pages beside him on the stair step. His heart outraced the rhythm of his pounding head as he sat there, trying to think things out. Dub would have to see these, he knew, but Dub had just left without saying much. He probably was home pouring another drink and crawling into the shower, then to bed again.

It had been a bad night for Brooks, a night of tossing and turning, a night of Sara spurning his erotic advances, a night in which he finally had given up on her and moved into the guest bedroom for two hours of restless sleep and then relentless, unwanted wakefulness as light dawned on the Sunday morning. He had finally slipped back into sleep around eight and woke up at two o'clock, as Sara ushered Dub out the front door.

He had stood at the top of the stairs, calling out a weak good-bye to Dub, and had sat on the top step holding his head in his hands. Sara moved around below, walking into the kitchen, he thought to prepare some food. She emerged shortly and came upstairs, approaching him without saying a word. He shifted to one side, thinking she wanted to pass, then saw she was holding something out to him -- a roll of paper. It was second sheets, the kind of paper he used in his newspapering days before computers and cold type and four-color pictures on the front page of every edition.

"What's this?"

Brooks half expected to read some sort of ultimatum written by Sara, a decree ordering him out of her life after his terribly boorish, drunken behavior the previous night. But Sara was not chiding him, nor was she ordering him out. She sat next to him on the steps as he unrolled the pages and began to read.

When he finished, he took Sara's hand, kissed it and said: "Will you ever forgive me?"

"Of course," she said. "I'm just still rattled about the trip home. And this note, which, yes, I did read, disturbs the hell out of me."

"Why? It may mean we can locate the murderer and get this thing over with."

She looked at him, doubt in her eyes. "Are you really so hung over, or is it you just have no concern for your safety?"

"What do you mean?"

Tears welled up in Sara's eyes.

Brooks drew her close. "What do you mean, baby?"

"Oh, Brooks! Last night, all night, I had these terrible dreams. I think someone was trying to kill you. Whoever was in that car last night was trying to get rid of you, don't you see?"

She shook with the crying, and Brooks held her tight.

"Let's hope not, Sara. Let's hope not."

He meant these words to ease her fears, but then he realized that his earlier speculation to Dub might not have been idle paranoia. Sara could be right. Someone could be after me, he thought. What to do now? Soothe her, for one thing, and resist the tendency toward his own anxiety, for another.

Where the hell was Harriet when he needed her? Atlanta, of course.

As he held Sara he hurt, mainly from too much liquor. The moment churned deep depression, and he felt that urge, too, to bury himself in sorrow, to sink quickly into the melancholy that brought him to Riverton, to his hometown and to the old school building where he lived. Was he really seeking something from the past when he moved into the schoolhouse or merely retreating into a guise of wistfulness? Self-doubt clouded these thoughts. What had he done in life, when had he won? And would he continue losing?

He thought this sadness born of hangover blues foolish. He looked down at Sara, nestled against his body on the top step, held her as she stopped crying and rested in his arms. He felt her warmth and her breathing. He thought back a year to an office in an old restored building, an old house on Peachtree Road, where the trees shrouded a slate shingle roof, on land that had predated -- and then survived -- Sherman's belligerence and the money-grubbing greed of decades of real estate developers. A house turned into the solitude of a psychologist's office, where rooms softly lit, Persian rugs and French tapestries helped assure quiet and solitude. Where one sank into soft, overstuffed sofas. Where these trappings cushioned the surgical procedure on one's inner self: Cut open, drawn out and carefully assembled in bloody mind pools through words splattering off a self-mirror. Where Brooks Sheffield climbed out of the cave of sadness and despair. He thought back to a time of near self-destruction and the slow unloading of the weapon, which still lay in a drawer or closet shelf, somewhere, deep within him.

"What is it about this school, this inanimate structure, that draws you?"

"I can't really say. It's hard to put into words. There are things about the school, though, that reach beyond its brick walls. It's personal. Memories seem to come alive for me, whether I'm in the building or not."

"Have you been there recently?"

"Yes, in the last two years."

"Tell me about that."

"I went there after my father died. I spent two weeks in Riverton to be there with him. He was very sick. We've talked about that. It was all a terrible time. Jane had died the year before, almost a year exactly. I was all alone, isolated and devastated the first hours after he died. I shirked the responsibilities of the older brother, so my brother Charles made all the arrangements. I had just been through all that with Jane's death. Loss was becoming difficult and hard to face up to. And it was coming too often.

"After leaving the hospital, I drove around an hour or so. In the evening I passed the old high school. I parked the car in back of the building, got out and tried one of the doors. It wasn't locked. Someone was having a meeting in the building, so I walked right in. I walked all over it. Had a good cry on the second floor landing, next to the home economics rooms and my eighth grade homeroom. Then I got up and went to the auditorium, took a seat on the back row, and just sat there for two or three hours. When I left, the building was locked. It took some doing to get out of there. But when I did, I felt better about things and myself.

"I did a lot of thinking about the past. I remembered one time in the auditorium. I was in the sixth grade and was overweight back then. People always picked on me, and I was really defensive. I was in the auditorium setting up chairs and music stands for an assembly program, a band concert. I played the tuba. The band director's mother sat in the back of the auditorium waiting for the program to start. No one else was there. Just us two. It was hot, and I was sweating, moving around the stage, setting up everything. She looked at me and said, 'What's wrong with you young man? Didn't you eat your breakfast this morning?' That was all she said. Doesn't mean much, but to me it was a kind, backhanded compliment. To me she was saying, 'You aren't sweating because you are fat and out of shape, but because your mother didn't feed you a proper meal.'

"I sat there and remembered that day, along with other times spent in the auditorium and in the school. I didn't feel sad or destroyed in that building the night my father died. I didn't feel whole either. But I did feel calm and less alone. I did feel that I was OK. And I didn't worry about a damned thing. If you can capture that, not being sad all the time and not wanting to die and not dreading life and death, then that's where you ought to be. Isn't it?

"So I'm going back. To the town, the old schoolhouse, where I left a lot of me. I may not become part of that former life, but I might find something worthwhile there."

The psychologist glared at Brooks in silence for a moment. Then he asked, "How do you think you will do that?"

"That I do not know, either. My mind has been turning it over and over, though."

"I feel you are saying you would like to go back to another time. We've covered this before. Have you thought about finding some of the people you knew then?"

"Yes. I can't imagine any of these people extending themselves to me now in a way that would help. I know I could renew some friendships. But people change. I'm not terribly interested in seeing other people as they are now, as they have changed, as they have manipulated their lives into the same destruction as I have mine. I have to find something about myself, something that was lost sometime ago. I can't say right now how I lost my self."

"Are you really thinking about going back?"

"Yes. I don't know when, though. Pretty soon."

Later Sunday afternoon, around five-thirty, Brooks left Sara at her house and drove toward Dub's. He brooded, receding into a soft complacency. Too, he still felt the liquor's residual effect, even though his headache, with the help of a painkiller, had diminished. He remembered feeling like this on Sunday evenings as a boy: The drugged sleepiness after awakening from those Sunday afternoon naps the whole family took. He thought, too, about the leftover meals at Sunday supper, which usually consisted of cold fried chicken, watery string beans and hard biscuits. He had consumed the chicken, often with a warmed-over biscuit, and avoided the string beans. While his mother was living, she served leftover chicken almost every Sunday supper. Later, the cook being off on Sundays, the three men -- Brooks, his brother and their father -- ate out for Sunday dinner and made do with sandwiches for supper. Today, he had no thoughts about his supper. He wasn't hungry. Sara had prepared a huge midafternoon breakfast, after they read the startling note.

Brooks left Sara's house intending to drive to Dub's, but he didn't go there directly. The reality of last night hung heavy. His friend Dub Campbell, dependable as always, faltered now in weakness and frailty from the bottle, his skills on the college gridiron gone. His strength now lay only in his size, now that the iron-fashioned muscles were memories in the flab of his upper arms.

How would Dub react to the note? And what would he say and do? Brooks had no idea. He wanted to give Dub plenty of time to recover from a bad drunk.

He followed a route around town similar to the ones taken a thousand times as a teenager, first proceeding from the east end of town to the west, then north and south on Houston Avenue, through the rich end and poor. Finally, he headed north again on the Moultrie highway, returning to town on the toilet-paper road -- the first paved road in Piscola County. People in this small town had elevated leisurely town driving from a pastime to an art, one punctuated by quiet gossip and other soft conversation points during the drive, which could go on for hours.

It was uncertainty rather than boredom that caused his meandering. In forty-five minutes, a short time indeed, he had grown restless enough to convince himself that Dub by now would have slept it off -- or tried hair-of-the-dog cures. He pulled the car to a stop in front of his old friend's small frame house and sat there for a while, turning everything over in his mind, one more time.

His mission completed, Watt Miller spent a relaxing day at home Sunday. Almost. He cooked with Jenny, and after lunch they read the Sunday paper together before retiring to the master suite for their usual brief lovemaking, performed gently of late because of Jenny's concern for the baby inside her. Jenny went to sleep afterward, and Watt got up to read a new novel.

Still, all the time, deep down, he sensed lingering turmoil. Yes, he felt relieved that he had written the note and delivered it, the delivery being easier than he expected. He had approached Sara Compton's house carefully enough, around eleven-thirty. The back door was open and the kitchen light was on, so he walked right in and deposited the note in a place where it would be found easily. His uncertainty now rumbled from what might happen and whether, if Gabriel Wheeler were identified as the witness he'd mentioned in the note, the old man would direct the sheriff back to Watt.

Three hours later, Jenny came into the den and said she was calling her parents to tell them the news.

Back home to Savannah.

How wonderful.

Watt tensed. Things were moving pretty fast.

"Hello, Mother," Jenny said, her voiced cracking as she talked in a high, squeaky tone, the same as when she told him about the baby.

Watt stood up and went into the kitchen, waving off talking to his in-laws. After all, he could offer them nothing concrete about the move. He sat in the kitchen and listened to Jenny talk about the move, timing it with the baby -- "If we can, Mother, but we just don't know" -- and a variety of other premature notions passing through the phone line as her mother chattered.

Obviously full agreement and encouragement came from the other end of the line.

Watt's mind drifted. Through the doorway connecting the kitchen with the dining room, he could see through a window onto Houston Avenue... and Brooks Sheffield's blue Volvo drive by the house! By the time he reached the window, the car was continuing slowly south on Houston.

Watt breathed deeply. The gut feeling was churning up fast now. He put his hands to his face and rubbed his eyes. Then he went back into the kitchen, where Jenny's conversation with her mother continued abuzz.

"Well, this answers a lot of questions. And the man who wrote this probably can tell us some more," Dub said, setting down the heavy white mug of black coffee.

"Yes, but will he talk to us?" Brooks asked, pacing slowly across Dub's small living room.

"Us?"

"Yeah, you and me."

"Brooks, I have to take this to the sheriff. This ain't no 'you and me' and the good ol' days stuff here. I've got a duty, since he called me in on this case, and, hell, up to now I've given him nothing. Shit, one of his jacklegged deputies came up with more than me. He tracked down the alibi of the man we thought did it."

"What? You know who did it?"

"We thought we did. But I can't talk about it."

"Well, I don't know why in the hell you haven't told me all this."

"I've let you in on too much, really. And I'll tell you more about it soon as I take this to the sheriff."

"I think I ought to go with you. The note is addressed to me, and because of that he'll want to talk to me."

Dub paused, looking back down at the note. He rolled up the pages, which were becoming limp.

"Fair enough. Let's go."

They went to the courthouse and then to the sheriff's house before they spotted him in his cruiser, driving down Houston Avenue. Back at the courthouse, a half-hour session in Sheriff Johnson's office proved futile. Though he refused to speculate on the note, he kept it, storing the second sheets in a plastic envelope he locked in his desk.

"He's reluctant to talk around you, Brooks," Dub said on the way back to his house.

"I'm important to this case. He ought to loosen up a bit. And besides that, I'm on your side."

"Look. Give him until tomorrow. I'll go by there first thing in the morning and see what he's thinking. He'll talk to me. Hell, he has to. He knows the note's something. I think he's just a little pissed that he couldn't fully follow through on some other angles before now. The note opens up a lot of things."

"Let me guess. A sound alibi isn't so sound any more?"

"That, yes. And, like the note said, things are really pretty simple if you look at it like looking at duck."

"What do you mean?"

"Well, if something looks like a duck, walks like a duck and sounds like a duck, there is that off chance that even a skeptic could agree it may be a duck. I think we have a full-grown mallard here, friend." Dub cast a wry glance at Brooks as he stopped the car and put the gearshift in park.

"So, who's the duck?"

"I'll tell you tomorrow after I talk with the sheriff."

"Aw, come on, Dub. Who the hell is it?"

"Tomorrow." Dub fumbled with the keys hanging from the ignition, as if to signal an immediate end to the conversation and rush Brooks on his way.

Brooks didn't let it drop that easily. "Do I know this person? Could I have known this person growing up here? Would I recognize this person?"

"I have to speculate that, yes, you could know this person. In fact, you'll at least recognize the name. These are things we've talked about, so don't get a ten-penny nail sideways up your butt over them. Tomorrow, we can discuss this in full, I promise. I feel certain I can convince the sheriff to go on a hunch I have, and if so, we may be able to start closing this thing down. But some things have to move. For one, we're going to talk to the phantom who wrote that note, and for another, we're going to talk with his witness. We'll break one of them to get the evidence on our man, our Florida leisure lifer, because I'm convinced he did this."

"But... who..."

"Tomorrow. Count on it."

With that, Dub got out of the car, leaving Brooks sitting there, and went into his house and shut the door.

Frustrated, Brooks felt lonely all of a sudden. Now, the melancholy that followed a hard drunk had sunk in quite well. It was time he got back, he knew that. He got into his car and drove to a phone booth to tell Sara that he was spending the night at his apartment at the school.

In 1969, Brooks Sheffield, fresh from a two-year stint in Washington working for his congressman, returned to Georgia and took a job as a reporter for The Atlanta Journal. With this move, after a courtship that spanned years and one whose beginnings were in junior high school, Brooks married

Jane Hudson. They said their vows in Riverton and honeymooned at the King and Prince Hotel on St. Simons Island.

The marriage bloomed into a wonderful life, except that it produced no children, a constant disappointment for both Brooks and Jane. They considered adoption but abandoned that course when the worst news came to them: Jane contracted cancer and believed, at first, she had a good chance to live. She didn't. Two years later and fourteen years into their marriage, Jane died.

By this point, what once had been Brooks' collegiate cheerfulness and optimism became dented in other ways: The declining health of his father, whose death followed Jane's, and the emotional meandering taken by his career as a newspaper editor, from hurt to anger to elation and pride in his work and then to hurt and anger again.

The end for Jane followed a terribly exhaustive physical trial of mostly lying in a hospital bed, barely living at all. She withered to skin and bones, lost her hair, all expression flat, colorless. The greatest loss was her laugh, along with the gentle way she would smile at Brooks when he gave her a dozen roses, a book or some other small gift. Those meant so much to her. Brooks brought her gifts every day or so after she became bedridden, and she sank as the days went by. With each gift the laughter sank, the smiles diminished and then her wonderful spirit of life died altogether. That was the hardest part: Seeing Jane's spirit die before her body surrendered. Jane's spirit, her love of living, touched Brooks in a very special way. When he saw this die, he lost hope for himself. Her body, her shell, lingering in paleness and without the beautiful natural blonde hair, took several more weeks to give up its fight. Jane's spirit died tragically and that was a terrible thing to see. In the end, her body had gone quietly, easing away.

Tonight, back at the school, he thought about Jane and his father and their deaths. He walked up the south stairs to the second floor, where Louie Basford was shot to death. He brought out his keys and unlocked the door to the attic steps. He walked up. There, in the attic that would have made such a wonderful place to live -- once fitted with plumbing and other human conveniences. There he sat on a paint drum and looked out the eye-shaped window to the town, settling now into night from the day's gloaming. The courthouse clock registered seven forty-eight. Brooks sat there observing the night, the children playing across the street, cars roaming about slowly, dogs meandering and barking and later several women walking home from the little Holiness Church two blocks north of the school.

It satisfied Brooks, this scene, from his seat perched on top of his world, he looked down on the parade of lives passing before him. Far from being a god, he possessed no control over anything before him, nor did he wish it. He did lay claim to a vantage point, however, and this grand vista allowed him entry into places no one else in the town enjoyed.

It was one in the morning when Brooks unseated himself from the perch above Riverton's slumber and plodded downstairs to his own bed.

Brooks left the schoolhouse the next morning but could not find Dub anywhere. He started driving around the courthouse several different times, passing Dub's house regularly, then called the courthouse for him. A sheriff's dispatcher said Dub had been in to talk with the sheriff earlier that morning but had left, and no one knew where he was. Next, Brooks tried the Valdosta GBI office. No word on Dub. And no, he had not been in there all morning, Brooks was told by a curt young woman who answered the phone.

The day remained briskly cold, as South Georgia winter can at times. He was glad he'd put on a thick wool sweater as well as a hunting jacket before leaving the school. Still, he was shivering in the heater-less Volvo, so he drove to Sara's house for coffee.

He stayed there for lunch. He told Sara about Dub's

reaction to the note, how much he resented hearing nothing else from Dub this morning, after he had promised to tell him everything. He called the courthouse again. No luck.

After lunch, he went back to the courthouse. Nothing. No car. No Dub. He drove out to the school to wait. I'll just sit here and let him find me, Brooks thought. Fat chance. He's ignoring me for some reason.

An hour later, around one-thirty, Dub banged on the heavy metal door to Brooks' classroom apartment.

"Dammit, boy, where the hell have you been?" Dub said, storming in.

"That's what I was screaming to myself about your whereabouts all day."

"Come on, we're taking a little trip. Got something to show you."

"OK," said Brooks, grabbing the hunting jacket and slipping into a pair of loafers.

Dub looked down.

"Oh no, not those sissy shoes," Dub said. "Get some boots on or something. We're heading for the woods."

Brooks went over to his makeshift closet and rummaged around under overcoats and three-button suits, finally dragging out a pair of old, black rubber Wellingtons.

"That's more like it," Dub said. He wore jeans, a long-sleeve navy blue sweatshirt, quilted parka and baseball cap, tan snake boots, heavily worn and scarred but oiled and well cared for.

Brooks sat down in a chair in the corner to put on his boots, then retrieved the old baseball cap he'd found in the school attic, the wooly, moth-eaten one.

"Well, I suppose you're ready," Dub said, looking Brooks over head to toe. "Let's go."

Outside, it had warmed some. Brooks immediately noticed Dub's new vehicle, a black Chevy Blazer with four-wheel-drive and a blue light mounted on the dashboard. The Blazer's oversized mud tires raised the vehicle high off the ground. Brooks managed to climb up and into the cab, sitting back on Dub's service revolver, in its holster and resting on the passenger seat.

"Damn, you're loaded and ready," he said as Dub got behind the wheel and started the engine.

"Always am," Dub replied, adjusting his crotch after landing heavily in the driver's seat.

Dub wheeled out of the sandy schoolyard and headed to the main highway leading west of Riverton. Two miles out of town, he turned left and proceeded along a winding dirt road to another paved road to the south. He crossed the southbound county road and stayed on the dirt trail deep into the woods. They drove past several hog pens and, in two or three more miles, came to a newly surfaced blacktop. Dub turned south on this road and stomped the accelerator.

Brooks sat silent, but he didn't have to broach the subject. Dub did all the talking. Several miles down the blacktop, as they headed for the Florida line, Dub told Brooks what they were doing.

"We're heading to a farm, which is about as close to the Florida line as you can get and still live in Georgia. It's owned by a fellow named Sam Warren, but I don't think he's there. At least, he wasn't there this morning."

"So, you've been there already?" Brooks asked.

"Oh yeah. Talked with the sheriff, and came out here with another agent. We snooped around through the woods, watching the house. Observing at this point. There's something I want to show you I think you'll be interested in."

"Sam Warren," Brooks mused aloud.

"Recognized the name?" Dub asked.

"Yeah. The Starlite Lounge."

"Yes, mister newspaperman. Haven't lost your touch completely. Boy, though, that day we were in there, I thought you had bled out your brain trying to sell it to science for the study of stupidity."

They crossed the Florida line and a mile later turned onto a narrow red clay road almost hidden at points by thick honeysuckle vines and small pines growing right up to the roadbed, what there was of it. Anyone driving this road's gray sand with less than a four-wheel would be foolish, for several times, even this big truck slid toward the bushes when they ran over a pot hole. Dub managed the steering effortlessly and held a steady course through the piney woods. Dub and the Blazer found high ground and soon left the low-lying pine brush for a wooded area crowded with oaks and other hardwoods. For a short time they drove along a narrow streambed.

"That the river that disappears?"

"Naught. It's a smaller river, a creek actually," Dub said. "It's just dried up. On downstream, there's a sinkhole that's pretty full right now, but this stream's been dry several years. Who knows, any month now, maybe this spring, it might perk up and flow again."

They left the streambed and drove back down into lower lying country, following narrow path along the firebreak of a cow pasture. Across the pasture Brooks saw Black Angus cattle grazing in the late winter sunlight. After a dip in the horizon, the tall obelisks of cypress, trunks with huge bottoms rising out of the water, marked a small pond where more cattle waded and drank.

"We just drove into Florida. That's one of the biggest Angus ranches in the northern half of the state," tour guide Dub informed his friend.

Brooks gazed out the window, saying nothing.

"Time to head back north," Dub said, immediately turning the steering wheel hard to the left.

They headed off the pasture-side road and into the woods. Surprisingly, they hit a hardtop within half a mile and stayed on it for several hundred feet before turning off to the right, again onto a narrow dirt road.

"All this backyard meandering is to get us as close to where we're going as possible without tipping our hand, should the subject be home," Dub told him.

Not a hundred feet off the hardtop, Dub slowed into a stand of oaks, pulling into the bushes, then hit reverse and turned back into the dirt road. Forward six or eight feet, reverse again, and he backed as far as he could into the bushes branches scraping the Blazer's paint and bending small trees beneath the oversized back bumper.

Dub snapped the holster to the backside of his western belt and jumped out of the cab. Brooks followed, pushing hard to open the door against bending branches and vines.

"So much for a quick getaway," Brooks said.

Dub looked over at him without remarking.

They walked up the sandy road, deep into the woods and a long way from the open pastures they had skirted earlier. Two, maybe two and a half miles later, both men breathing hard and sweating, Dub stopped and sat down. Catching his breath, he talked in a rough whisper. Brooks leaned in close and heard him well.

"Two hundred feet over there, through those trees, is Sam Warren's farm. We're going to walk around the backside of a small pasture backing up to his barn and house. There's a fair sized pigpen off to the north side of the house beneath some pecan trees. We're going to work our way around far enough to see if Mr. Warren is home and for you to look around, because, like I said, there's something I want you to see."

On the drive down, Brooks had resisted pressing Dub for information, even though he wanted to do so. Obviously, Dub had brought him in on something, so Brooks was satisfied to see what developed; he was certain he would find out a great deal on this ride to the Florida line with Dub Campbell.

They rested a minute or two more, then headed through the woods quietly. The pasture appeared. Across the grass, perhaps four hundred yards away, a small white-frame farmhouse stood. There was a tool shed of weathered wood behind the house and, as Dub had described, a nearly dilapidated barn leaned slightly near what appeared to be a pigpen.

A truck parked on the pasture side of the structure

caught Brooks' eye immediately. He remembered reading Sherlock Holmes stories as a boy, then going to the Ibex movie theater in Riverton and watching Basel Rathbone and Nigel Bruce bring the characters and scenes to life, just as he had imagined them. If that was exciting, real danger was the sensation now. Seeing the truck brought the note to life. Still, his senses on full alert, he felt as though he were somehow part of a movie, one in which they were very close to solving the crime.

"See what I mean?" Dub said.

"That's the truck! The truck in the note!"

"Shhh! If it ain't we're talking one just like it."

"Has to be. Look, how many pig farmers in Piscola County are still driving thirty-year-old pickups?"

"Plenty, probably. But that ain't the point."

"Yeah?"

"The point is, the man who owns and drives this pickup used to employ the late Louie Basford."

"Did Louie work at the Starlite?"

"No. Shhh. Tell you later. Look."

The door to the farmhouse opened and out came a large green plastic garbage can. White arms attached to the can emerged, then the perky figure of a pretty young woman dressed too skimpily for the weather in tight short-shorts and a halter-top. A large gold bracelet dangled loosely from her right wrist and nearly covered her hand. Her hair was cut in a bob, points falling sharply across her cheeks, and the back trimmed close in an abrupt taper up the back of her head. She dragged the garbage can down the three back steps and set it next to some other boxes that appeared to also hold trash and garbage. She glanced around the yard, shivered, wrapped her hands tightly across her bosom, and hurried lively back into the house. The door slammed shut.

"Think he's there?" Brooks whispered.

"Doubt it. His big Cadillac isn't there. At least, not that I could see this morning."

They stayed close to the house, first by walking a flank

to the property through the woods and going nearly to the main road that ran in front of the house. From this vantage point at the south side of the house, they had a clear picture of the front yard and a better view of the hog pen across the drive.

Why, Brooks thought, did so many farmers place their pigpens close to their house and next to the road?

They waited, but there was no Cadillac and no other activity. One or two cars passed on the road. They worked their way back toward the house and waited nearby, out of sight.

The pretty woman apparently enjoyed soap operas or sleeping or reading, because they saw no more of her for the next two hours. They gave up the watch at five o'clock and retreated back into the woods, down the long sandy path to the Blazer and the trip back home, which followed an equally circuitous but shorter route than the drive down earlier in the afternoon.

On the way, Dub told Brooks about Sam Warren and the eagle eyes now observing the old man every time he went to Florida.

Chapter 11 - Crystal

The day after the morning after energized Brooks Sheffield. While he'd had little rest the last two nights, having spent most of Monday waiting and then moving fast, when he'd finally gotten home he crashed down like a big pine tree falling. He slept like a baby -- for a while. The afternoon activity of hiking through the woods, squatting, waiting, sweating in the cold and hiking back to the truck had worn him out.

Dub had dropped him off at the school just before six. He had gone inside, pulled off the hunting jacket, Wellingtons and his shirt, and collapsed on the bed. He woke up after a few hours thinking of Sam Warren, about Dub's investigation and how the law's tentacles were slowly pulling in pieces of information about him.

He knew from Dub that Sam had kept a low profile for many years as he became involved in both the questionable and the criminal. Lately he had become ubiquitous, popping up in the company of others being watched for their unlawful activity.

Sam had made nocturnal trips to Tallahassee to escape Riverton and sink into anonymity. Those trips actually had catapulted him into the eyes of the eagle, eyes seeing everything and recording everything for reference. Sam had appeared, at first, an unknown to those eyes, an ancillary figure who possibly had stumbled into bad company; now they ranked Sam as one of the crowd. The eagle punched his name through the state law enforcement system's computers and other databases where business licenses, car registrations and a variety of other information unfolded, and then began interviewing his former associates.

Now, a sheriff and GBI agent in Georgia were very

interested in Sam's whereabouts on the night of a murder. The eagle and its infrared gaze now pursued Sam Warren. Soon, very soon, the eagle would drop for its prey.

Brooks thought back over the years. He searched every wisp of childhood recollection, but he could not remember one thing about Sam Warren. He'd once known a boy in his class whose father owned a pool hall in another town, but that was completely unrelated. Sam Warren's name stirred nothing in Brooks Sheffield.

He tried to read, couldn't, and after a while, slept fitfully. Images came to him, rolling into his mind and rocking his body. Everything seemed in motion -- his bed, the covers, the pillows under his head, so that with sheets winding around his legs, he felt captured.

The images rushed, sometimes too real.

He woke up long enough to wander to the bathroom and urinate. A flush and he stumbled back toward the bed.

The dreams drifted back.

This time it was hair, reddish black, blowing in a soft breeze. No, not a breeze, a woman's hair bouncing as she runs across a field. This beautiful woman, hair in a bob cut, her red lips glowing their natural color in the sunshine. As she runs barefoot across the field, her light cotton dress flies out and up, baring beautiful white thighs, bouncing with her breasts with the beat of feet hitting the ground, lifting and reaching into the run. The beautiful woman, who has the youthful look of a girl, runs down the hill, the reclining side of a pasture, toward a swamp and cypress trees. She laughs as she runs. He's running with her, then after her, darting over cow pies and muddy spots in the grass. She teases him in a challenge to catch her, to catch her and have her by the swamp at the bottom of the hill.

Her laughter turns to screams. She's falling now, falling down the hill, rolling through the cow pies and muddy brown, not green, grass. She's falling in a roll toward the swamp, what was a pond filled with black water. He runs after her, but he sees now her falling is her attempt to escape from him. She screams from the fear that he will catch her and violate her, by the swamp at the bottom of the muddy, brown-grass pasture. Cows close in, mooing and trampling the earth.

Brooks sees himself as the man, the pursuer, chasing her. He turns ghoulish in his thoughts while watching as the man, he thinks himself, stops above the girl as she splashes on hands and knees through the black swamp water. She turns to face the evil thing, who steps slowly into the water. She screams again, and continues fighting through the black water as the thing marches after her into the water. The girl splashes through blackness.

Brooks stumbles in the dream and falls. His last glimpse of the girl, he thinks, comes when she disappears into the swamp water. He's not sure about this. He's not sure at all. He drifts and moves on through sleep.

He woke up late Tuesday afternoon. It was a sunny winter day, seasonably cold, down into the thirties. Brooks saw clear blue sky when he opened the beige drapes on the basement window into the apartment. From low in the western sky out over the schoolyard came slanting rays of sun, brightening the former classroom, transforming it in glaring contrasts of golden light and shadows.

Brooks sat in a chair opposite the door and the window, reading Will Durant's The Age of Reason Begins. He'd been plumbing the depths of this volume off and on for some fifteen years, concentration never coming easily. He heard, and tried to dismiss, a slight tapping -- no, a clicking -- outside the window, across the schoolyard.

He kept on reading. The sun's rays seemed to fade with every passing second, and as the room grew dim, the clicking became louder.

Click. Click. Click. Click, click. Click. Click. Click. Click, click.

A stride, a stop, a turn. Stride back, stop, turn and repeat.

Brooks' hand lifts a corner of the beige drape and he looks out onto the schoolyard. He brings his other forearm up to shield the sun's light, which although dimming still shines with some brilliance. He pans the schoolyard as if he's making a movie. The clicking sounds are off to his left. He sees her walking, step by step and back and forth, alongside the old field house.

Her hair is cut in a bob, shining dark black-red in the sun, her lipstick bright red. She steps out of the roofline shadow and into the light of the brilliant but fading sun's rays. She looks across the schoolyard for something. Perhaps a ride, a companion late in picking her up. But from what? What was this young woman doing here? Brooks can't tell.

He stares at her, watches her go back and forth. Click, click, click. Click, click. Back and forth. The sound of her pacing suggests impatience, but as Brooks looks at her there seems nothing about her manner to signal irritation that her ride, her companion, has not yet arrived.

She stops, looks again. Both ways. Brooks looks out across the schoolyard, then back toward the building's corner, which hides, for him, her view to the Southside street. Suddenly, it occurs to Brooks that she is waiting for no one in particular; she's just cautiously gauging the moment, the right moment when she will not be seen walking across the schoolyard from the old field house to the school -- and to his door.

Here she comes. She's walking to his room. She looks his way.

The drape drops. He awaits the knock.

The steps come closer, muted by the gravel and sand of the schoolyard, then clicking again on the cement sidewalk leading up to the school and his door.

Tap, tap, tap comes the knock. He moves across the room and opens the door.

Bright red lipstick shines forth in his first look at this woman, this young woman who takes off black sunglasses to reveal her eyes piercing into his.

Her wan smile dissolves quickly. She looks at him with dark eyes.

He sees arching eyebrows, freckles pecking through light makeup. Asian? He wonders, as he says, "Come in," without hesitating.

She nods and enters. She wears a short black skirt, and the neckline of her deep purple blouse plunging along a gold chain lavaliere of a snake. Plenty of flesh showing, and he sees breasts of average size. The long single-strand gold necklace dangles into the deep cleavage. Her ear lobes are studded with tiny diamonds, linked by a tiny silver chain. Pearl bracelets wrap her left wrist while a thick, four-inch-wide gold bracelet buries her right. She wears no rings, he notices as she walks in, clasping and unclasping her hands in a methodical fashion.

His eyes follow her down the six steps into his classroom-bedroom. At the bottom of the steps, she turns and faces him.

"What are you looking for?" Brooks asks.

She laughs a silly, sarcastic laugh.

"Well, I wondered when you might say something or ask that question." She continues to smirk. "Perhaps it would be appropriate for me to introduce myself. I'm Crystal Durrough, and you're Mr. Sheffield, I believe."

"Yes. Brooks Sheffield."

"Mind?" She turns toward the sideboard and nods a glance at the bottles sitting atop the old piece of furniture.

"But, yes. I'm sorry, I should offer you something."

Brooks loosens up. "Scotch, gin?   What's you're pleasure, Miss Durrough?"

"Scotch and water, please."

He goes over to pour. "I have to tell you I don't get many visitors." He looks back at her as he unscrews the cap.

"No?" She cracks a quick smile, otherwise maintaining

a gesture of seriousness.

"Won't you sit down?"

Crystal Durrough sits on the corner of Brooks' bed and crosses her elegant legs, right over left, with the left toe barely touching the floor.

"Since you don't get many visitors, you must be floored by my presence, Mr. Sheffield. Or, may I call you Brooks?" the woman says, rimming the drink glass with a finger as if to clean it, then taking a sip.

Brooks nods. "Yes, you may. I'm curious as to why you're here," Brooks says, taking his own drink of gin.

The woman looks at him. And Brooks looks at her. Her beauty was plain but deep. Her confidence was overwhelming.

"Let's imagine for a moment that I'm interested in real estate."

"You're an agent, then?"

She holds her gaze on him.

"I said, let's imagine."

"OK. Guess I can go along with that."

"And let's suppose I am representing a client who wants to acquire this old schoolhouse," she says, pausing on the word "acquire" as if to choose and emphasize it carefully.

"Oh. I see."

"Supposing those things were true, I'm curious to know how you might react to a possible... a possible proposition that could lead to your disposing... rather, selling this piece of property."

"Imagining all those things," Brooks says, "might logically lead to my thinking you really would want to buy this old building. Imagining all that you say, however, I couldn't say that I would give it a second thought."

Her eyebrows arched higher, bringing the penciled peaks to two craggy points. She looks wide-eyed, either in anticipation of his continuing or of an explanation on what he had just said.

"I imagine that thinking it through would be well worth

your time and consideration, Brooks."

"Well. I mean, imagine along with me for a moment," Brooks says. "Consider that I've not lived here long. I enjoy it and I haven't entertained leaving. Or selling it. Imagine that, if you will?"

After a pause, the woman glances down to the glass and says: "I see."

Then she reaches over and sets her drink on the floor and in the movement her blouse drops loose, revealing her breasts. She straightens up, pulling on the blouse's shoulders, having accomplished the effect she intended.

She gets up from the bed and walks over to Brooks, who stands by the sideboard.

"I just want you to also imagine this, Brooks. For a day or so. And I want this between you and me." She presses against him. "You're a nice looking man, Brooks. There are other things you should be free to imagine, too."

"Yes," Brooks says.

"No need to be nervous. Here, drink some gin."

Crystal Durrough takes Brooks' glass and offers it to him, and as she holds it, he takes a sip. She snuggles close to him. He feels her breasts and her right leg rubbing into his thigh.

"There are a great many things we can imagine together. And do. And enjoy. You know, we've just met, but since I came to Riverton a short while ago myself, I've heard a lot about you. There's something mysterious about a man who lives in an old abandoned schoolhouse. Something quaint and charming about it, too."

She puts the glass down, brings her arms around him and gently touches her nose, then her chin into his chest.

Brooks mellows through the drink and the attention this woman gives him.

"Sometime I'll give you a tour of the building, Miss Durrough."

"Fine. I would love to see it."

"But tonight wouldn't be the time. Too dark."

She chuckles. "Yes. It is a big, dark old building. And there are ghosts, I imagine, in a building this old."

She moves her hands down to his waist and fondles the leather of his belt.

He smiles at her and his desire for her builds.

"Ghosts and goblins and all sorts of things that go bump in the night. How could one live in an old haunted school? How could you sleep at night?"

"There are ways," he replies.

She closes her eyes and embraces him, rubbing her lips, her whole face into his chest and neck.

"I can just imagine some of the ways. Counting schoolbooks. Counting old girl friends," she says.

"Yes, and others I can imagine, too."

She kisses him hard and deep, and clutches his head in her hands as she speaks.

"Just imagine the things, Mr. Sheffield," she says. "Mmm, just imagine..."

Brooks slept on in the chair, not noticing the Durant tome slip heavily into his lap. Jane came to Brooks that night, too, took him by the hand and pulled him into the school's hallway next to the lunchroom.

Neither one of them says anything, as they stand in front of a locker and then, suddenly, they are outside. It's cold and snowing, and a low cloud cover hangs in the night above them. Jane and Brooks float as they walk. She leads him up the steps to the front entrance of the school on the first floor. They walk inside, close the doors and stand there, staring out the tall front double doors and down onto the sidewalk below. That snow covers the ground is unusual, almost unheard of in South Georgia.

In the distance, the courthouse clock glows. The cupola housing the clock shines brightly, too. Brooks sees something different about the cupola. Its gold dome radiates light from within, some unseen internal source.

Together, they turn toward the main hallway of the school and stand before the trophy case, which is filled with gold sporting figures, silver cups, banners, rotting sport jerseys, old footballs and nearly deflated basketballs. Several baseball bats lean into a corner. Most of the game objects, the balls, bats and jerseys, have writing on them. The writing glows in the dark.

One oversize football proclaims: "Riverton 29, Commerce 16 -- 1948 Class BB State Championship." Nearby is the state trophy from that year.

A yellowing black-and-white photo from the 1950s hangs in the case. The picture shows Georgia Tech football Coach Bobby Dodd signing up Riverton's star quarterback, Judd Worley, in 1954. Coach Dodd and Worley's parents are smiling, but the young Worley looks serious as he puts pen to paper for the photographer.

A Confederate flag, a gift to the school by the local U.D.C. chapter, shrouds a portion of the case. A fading, handwritten letter, framed underneath the flag, reads: "The banner the Piscola Volunteers carried into war. These brave boys held it high, never faltering in their resolve. This legacy we do hereby pass on to all the young men and women of The Riverton Schools. May you hold your heads and hearts high no matter the joy or the struggle that awaits you in life. Given this day, April 23, 1918. The United Daughters of the Confederacy."

In the center of the cabinet, near the Bobby Dodd picture, is a retired jersey from the 1959 football squad. The jersey belonged to Grant Neely, who died in a car crash on the Piscola Road. Jane points to a more permanent memorial to this young man, and she and Brooks float over to study the bronze plaque mounted onto the wall at the entrance to Graystone High. They walk through the first-floor halls through fog and time. The silent snow falls past the open windows throughout the school.

It's 1914. The first class of five people is graduating

from Graystone High School. The four girls are getting dressed in puffy gowns in the library storage room. Outside the principal's office is a young man dressed in his Sunday best. The talk of parents, teachers and others who have gathered around is the success of the school's first year and the grand achievement this class, though small, has made. The boy looks nervous and out of place as the girls emerge. The entire group walks up the step to the auditorium where others from the community have gathered for the ceremony. A piano starts playing as the graduates ascend the stairs, around the corner into the fog and out of sight.

Jane and Brooks follow them to the second floor, where all have disappeared. They find nothing but dark in the second floor auditorium, no commencement processional, no arts matrons, no pianos or violins playing. They follow the long hall to its south end, to a light shining through a classroom window. Jane and Brooks walk toward the light, coming from the gymnasium. As they near the windows to look out, they hear crowds cheering. Snow covers the ground and the roof of the shell. The crowd cheers as feet stomp on the floor. One hears a basketball being dribbled down the court, the running of players from one end to the other. The crowd erupts in cheers as one team scores. Then the blaring buzzer calls halftime to this game, played in 1933. Doors open, and for a short while the game takes a breather. The excitement diminishes, and some spectators emerge onto the snow. Men in white shirts and heavy coats pull out and light up cigarettes and talk about the game and the weather and agree their team was bound to win. Something needs to lift their spirits from the torment of the Depression and no jobs and no sign of any. And the weather, the unusual weather of bleakness and snow.

Brooks and Jane look out the window. The game resumes, and as second-half play builds to a peak, the gym's lights fade. The cheering grows softer, the glow dies away, and the hulk of a building slowly disappears into the gray of night and the shimmering white of snow.

Jane and Brooks drift back and float down the dark, second-floor hall. It's 1943, they know, as they walk to the north end of the hall, toward the home economics classroom. There are voices in a room, the teacher's lounge. Jane and Brooks creep up and listen.

"No, Sammy, careful now."

Jane and Brooks see a young woman, who is wearing an oversized letterman's sweater and a dress that's pulled up nearly to her waist. Her white socks are pulled low over saddle oxfords. She seems to be embracing, then wrestling with a young man. They only see him from the back.

"Let's just kiss. Kiss me, Sammy. Not there. Kiss my lips."

The young man doesn't speak. He clasps his hands and arms around her.

"No, Sammy, stop. I'm not ready. No," cries a young woman.

She pushes and tries to shove him off or herself away. He pins her to the teacher's lounge sofa. She manages to free a hand and slaps him clumsily on one ear. He pauses, then raises a fist and punches her in the chest. She screams, and he wraps a hand over her mouth then claps a forearm across her neck. He moves his free hand to her leg. The young woman cries hysterically. He relishes in winning the struggle.

In typical Jane fashion, she moves a hand over Brooks' eyes and with a tug on his arm pulls him away from the scene.

The fog drifts into Brooks' face. Jane holds her hand steady over his eyes, guiding his every step as they walk along,

She lifts her hand and there they are, dancing to a slow one at their Junior-Senior Prom. Jane wears a gown; Brooks a white sport coat. They dance only a moment before the fog envelops them again, Jane lets go, and Brooks floats by himself. He realizes her absence and reaches out for her. Jane isn't there. He tries to call her and cannot speak.

He run-floats into the fog. He stumbles without Jane

there to guide him through its thickness, and he falls... a hole in the cloud... a hospital bed.

Jane lies there, emaciated, in the sweater and skirt she wore in the yearbook picture. Her expression is just like that picture, but she's skin and bones, and she has no hair. Hard nipples protrude through the flimsy, moth-eaten sweater. The skirt is ripped and wrinkled. Her feet are bare and scarred and tangled in dried swamp grass and mud.

Brooks approaches the bed. Jane looks up at him, her eyes bulging in fright and pain. He reaches out to her and walks toward the bed. She tries to raise an arm. Her eyes have a longing. She wants him near her. Near-skeletal hands reach for her neck and raise a pearl necklace. She struggles to undo the necklace and hand it to him. As she does, her gold wedding band and diamond fall from a bony finger.

Brooks tries to call out to her, but no sound comes. Tears roll out of Jane's eyes, then she smiles, trying hard to muster the strength to keep holding the necklace out to him.

Brooks struggles and falls. He screams for Jane, but looking back he sees nothing of the bed or her above him as he tumbles down into the depths of the fog. He falls into blackness.

The morning glow from the window jolted Brooks awake early, perhaps seven o'clock. Stiff, he sat in the chair a moment and thought about the dreams. Disturbing dreams. He shook loose the thought and gained sight of the day's reality. No, just silly dreams.

He stood up. He and Dub were going to meet with the newspaper editor, Watson Jennings Miller IV. A pretentious name by anyone's standard, Brooks thought as he started to dress.

Silly dreams.

Chapter 12 - The Herald

For the last one hundred years, at least, the glass front doors to The Riverton Herald had rattled the signal of a caller. Heads turned when the rattling ushered in the visitor. The sound meant a momentary stop in the workday and gave time to observe if the visit were routine, someone placing a small ad, renewing a subscription or simply buying a copy of the paper. Occasionally the doors' clatter announced an important figure -- one of the town's prominent citizens or politicians, a major advertiser or, the inevitable heavy yoke every small-town editor carries, an angry reader wanting to vent his quarrel with the editor. No matter the grievance or contentious and often outrageous behavior of the person delivering it, any visitor's business held importance, if to no one but themselves.

Wednesday morning was a bad time for anyone to drop by. It was the day Watt Miller rushed to get the paper out, and by early afternoon he would have to be on his way to the printing plant in neighboring Valdosta. Wednesdays meant the one late night Watt always had to work.

Watt's visitors were not unaware of the paper's production schedule when they arrived just as this Wednesday began to rush forward.

Dub Campbell came in first, and Watt was just turning his head around toward the door when Brooks Sheffield followed. Neither man offered greetings to the office staff, beyond a suggestion of a nod from Brooks. They looked directly at Watt, then walked right past him into his office and sat down.

Alarmed, Watt followed them in. He was so nervous he could feel his heart pounding, his mouth going dry. He tried to give nothing of this away. He failed.

Dub did most of the talking. He came to the point, drawing little from a GBI academy class on interviewing skills and much from his years of conducting what sometimes was the crucial first, and often fruitful, questioning of a suspect.

"Mr. Miller, I believe you know me. I'm Dub Campbell of the Georgia Bureau of Investigation, and you should know Mr. Sheffield here," Dub said, reaching into his jacket pocket and pulling out several sheets of paper, folded. "Wonder if you could tell me if you wrote this note?"

Dub unfolded the copies and handed them over to Watt Miller. Brooks saw shaking hands take the pages and a twitch of a lip in reaction to it.

For a moment, Watt seemed to be reading the missive page by page. Then, resigned to reality, he dropped his arms to the chair and looked Dub in the eye. In a voice that cracked on several words and seemed to be on the verge of breaking completely, Watt said in a strained whisper: "Look here. Yes, I wrote this. But I can't talk about it here. Can we ride up the street?"

"Sure. Let's go," Dub said.

"If you'll wait one minute. I have to give these stories and ads to someone. Today's the day the paper gets out, so I can't be away for long. I have to get these over to the printer."

Dub nodded reluctantly and watched as Watt Miller, the country newspaper editor, jerked up from his desk chair and hurried over to a middle-aged woman in the main office area. He spoke quickly in low tones to her, apparently explaining he was being called out and would she take the package of copy to the printer. The woman, Mrs. Pinson, seemed puzzled by Watt's instructions. When he finished, she grimaced, reached for her purse and went out the door with the package, mumbling something to a young woman at the reception desk.

Dub and Brooks stood up then, and the three men left, offering no explanation to the confused receptionist.

They climbed into Dub's big Chevy Blazer and rode over

to Graystone High School. They went inside, to the auditorium, near the spot where Sam Warren shot Louie Basford, and talked in private. They covered the entire note and everything else Watson Jennings Miller IV had to tell, and by the time they finished, Watt Miller had missed his deadline. Dub and Brooks got the impression he didn't care. They dropped him off at The Herald office having heard it all, including Miller's reasons for writing the note and his decision to leave town and the newspaper business for good. Now they would turn their attention to Sam Warren.

"We ought to talk with Gabriel Wheeler right away," Dub said as they drove back toward Warren's farm. "But I want to concentrate on keeping an eye on Warren. If we have to we can sit down with Wheeler in a day or so, although I think we have enough on Warren right now."

"Anything from your friends in Florida?"

Dub had told Brooks about his contacts with law enforcement officers in Tallahassee and Orlando. He had filled them in on the murder in Riverton, on Sam Warren and his business interests. As it turned out, Dub's information investment paid off quickly. Almost immediately, a Florida contact had let him know that Sam Warren's name was listed in a criminal investigation around drug smuggling and that Sam had been seen recently in some interesting company.

Sam Warren's empire, which he had guarded so carefully for forty-five years, had begun to crumble.

"They think Sam Warren might be in on a prostitution ring out of Tallahassee, but they can't tie anything to him. He's been spotted escorting a woman named Charlotte Welles. The Florida boys think she's involved in running the ring. They noticed Sam while they were tailing her in Tallahassee earlier this year. You guessed it -- the weekend after Basford was shot."

"So she's his air-tight alibi."

"Well, Sheriff Johnson doesn't know this, but yes, a whore is Sam's alibi. Thing is, he claims he was in Tallahassee most of that week, but I feel certain he didn't go down there until after the shooting. Now, we know he probably didn't if his pickup is the same one Gabriel Wheeler saw. And let's just say there's a good to better-than-even chance it is."

"Where is Warren now?"

"Nobody knows. Sheriff has talked to all his main pool hall people and others in the county. They swear Sam's been out of town the whole week, in fact, a lot since Basford was killed."

"So why don't you and the sheriff go out and talk to the woman at his house?"

"Don't want to make too many waves. I think we're close to tying the knot on the Basford murder, but we don't want to screw up the bigger take -- a string of whorehouses he may be running from here to Tampa, along with the drugs."

"Well what if, say, she were to come to us?"

"How do you think that will happen?"

"It already has," Brooks said.

"What?" Dub turned toward Brooks, so amazed he forgot to steer -- until the big Blazer veered onto the rough gravel shoulder. He pulled it back. "What the hell...?"

"She came to visit me late yesterday. Stayed quite awhile. We talked. She wants, or rather her client wants to make an offer on the schoolhouse."

"Why didn't you tell me about this earlier?"

"No time." Brooks rolled his tongue nonchalantly under his lower lip and continued. "I had a pretty bad night of it, Dub. I really had to sort things out. And then I wanted to get the meeting with Miller out of the way and hear what he had to say."

"Let me get this straight," Dub said. "That slinky bitch we saw at Sam Warren's yesterday came to visit you last night?"

"Around six-thirty. It was still light."

"OK. OK. Spit it out. What did she say?"

"Basically it was real simple. She asked if I would entertain the notion of selling the school. And could she entertain me while I thought about it."

"Huh?"

"She's a first-class operator. Very confident. Very commanding of the situation. She walks in, introduces herself, and asks for a drink. She struts her stuff, not overtly, but struts no less. She sits down on the bed, crossing her legs, leaning over to reveal lovely, though not ample, wonders. Then you begin to balk. And when you do, she shifts toward a softer, more persuasive manner. She moves in close, touches softly and talks gently. I imagine that as call girls go, she's one of those thousand-dollar-a-night 'escorts,' as they call them in Atlanta."

"You fucked her?"

"That doesn't matter," Brooks said, reading the wonder in Dub Campbell's voice, "but, in a word, no."

"Did she mention Warren's name?"

"Of course not."

"She say anything that would hint she saw us, or someone, out at Warren's place yesterday?"

"Not a word or a hint."

"And what time did she drop by?"

"As I said, six-thirty or so. I was trying to get some sleep. Anyway, the sun was beginning to go down. Sunlight poured through those big windows in my room. The drapes were drawn. I'm reading when I hear this clicking sound. First thought it was a cricket. Then I thought it was some kid outside was clicking one of those metal crickets you find in Cracker Jacks. Then, I don't know, it was a strange scene, but I kind of felt somebody else was outside, somebody other than kids playing. It didn't occur to me that the noise, the clicking, was coming from someone walking in high heels. Not until I looked out the window."

"She was right outside?"

"No, across the schoolyard on that stretch of cement sidewalk in front of the field house."

"She park there or what?"

"No, I didn't see a car. Guess she parked on the street."

"How about when she left? Hear a car?"

"No. Didn't think about it."

"Don't imagine you did, after what she did to you. Or might have done." Dub said that grinning.

"She left around nine-thirty, and I went to sleep."

"And you didn't look out after she left or hear anything?"

"Nope."

"Boy. Some detective you are. Some ex-newspaperman, too. You miss the obvious opportunities."

"What's the big deal?"

"The deal is, what if Sam Warren drove her there? What if she drove his pickup? What if he were waiting the whole time? What if he wandered around the school, poking around while you poked her, or didn't poke her, or whatever you did or didn't do with her for three hours?"

"None of that happened."

"You don't know that. You were plying her with booze. Did you go out into the school at any time?"

"No need to. First, I can hear everything in the school, and certainly I can hear people walking. Second, I didn't want her in the school, at least any place other than my room."

"Hmm." Dub considered this and had little more to say, a rarity for him, as he concentrated on the road ahead. This time he drove directly, more or less, to Sam Warren's farm. The day was much like that day before it, sunny, with a gentle coolness brought in the evening before, and nearly cloudless.

Dub picked up speed as they neared Sam Warren's house on the two-lane hardtop that curved in front of the farm. From a hundred yards away, Brooks could see the white house and the pigpen to the north side, the side they were coming in on, and the weathered barn. Soon they could see that no car was visible near the house. Dub broke his speed slightly in passing the house, and they both scanned the yard for the pickup without luck. This didn't surprise either of them since the truck could easily have been hidden to one side of the barn. No sign of the slinky woman. No sign of anything but pigs, a few chickens and a skinny dog.

The Blazer passed the house, with both Dub and Brooks craning their necks for a last glimpse. Dub had planned only one sweep by the house on the off chance that Sam Warren was inside and looking at the road. They had seen enough, anyway; no vehicles in sight, which meant Sam Warren was away.

They rounded the curve near the Florida line when the old pickup truck rolled to a stop on the dirt road running into the hardtop near Sam Warren's house.

Sam's eyes followed the big, black state-issued Chevy Blazer as it headed south. The two snoopy occupants of the truck were, no doubt, law enforcement officers, Sam Warren thought as he shifted into low gear and chugged slowly onto the hardtop for a ways before turning into his driveway.

The bitch didn't do so hot. And they're getting close.

Time for Sam Warren to get even once again.

He stopped the truck beside the barn, then turned and looked back at the road in front of his house.

He scowled a moment and broke into a hideously wicked laugh.

Watt Miller's bad day nosedived after his meeting with Dub Campbell and Brooks Sheffield.

At nine-thirty, the presses were only just getting ready to run with this week's edition of The Riverton Herald. Two-and-a-half hours late, and the press room would have to go overtime, calling in more help for the other weeklies that were now backed up and waiting on The Herald. What's worse, Watt and his father would have to pay hefty overtime charges for the press crew being called in.

Damn the business world, Watt thought, damn that smart-ass Brooks Sheffield and his overgrown bear buddy, the snoop.

Two hours at that schoolhouse had caused Watt Miller's nightmare. Mrs. Pinson had done her job less than adequately, dropping off the copy at the front of the printing plant and then leaving. There the last batch of copy for the week's edition sat until Watt arrived at four o'clock. Two hours behind schedule, the pressroom foreman, usually cordial to Watt, erupted. The paste-up artists and typesetters fumed, too. And all of them pointed a silent, unseen finger at him.

Watt had messed up. He should have never written the note, he told himself. He should have just walked out.

Nope. No chance of that now. They were getting ready to start the press, and in forty-five minutes to an hour, with no breakdowns, he would have the week's edition loaded, covered securely with a tarp and pulling out for Riverton. He could unload and be home by midnight. Maybe.

There were several last-minute adjustments to the press. Then it started, and slowly papers began rolling out onto the conveyor that took them to stacking and a loud machine that wrapped the papers in bundles of a hundred.   Watt reached onto the conveyor and picked up several copies. He took them aside, dropped them on a table and opened up one to skim, page by page, the product of his growing frustration and his day of hell.

After the cursory look, he turned back through, checking page numbers and making certain that every major ad, to his numbed memory of the hour, had found its allotted space. He soon finished, since The Herald of late contained few major advertisements.

He turned around, dropped back against the table and looked around him. The pressman speeded up, in a hurry now to get The Herald off so they could run the other papers' plates that were stacking up. The foreman ignored Watt now, concerned instead with make-ready for the next run. He looked at his watch.

Watt started loading papers just before ten when the first bundles began dropping off the binder. When the foreman and a mail room worker came over to help him load, the tension eased, even though the foreman broke away from the task two or three times to holler orders to the composing room and the pressmen.

By the time Watt was ready to leave, the foreman had disappeared and three relief pressmen had come in, none excited about the prospects of working overtime in the middle of a Wednesday night to print weekly newspapers. They entered knowing someone at sometime during the day had messed up. They looked at Watt and figured correctly, shaking their heads.

Watt left as soon as the last bundle was loaded. He secured the tarp quickly, leaving twine knotted loosely in several places.

Bye, bye press plant, he thought as he drove away. He figured he probably may only have to do this for another month or so. Not much longer. After that, he would be finished with late nights around inky pressrooms, the smart talk of the young, blue-collar women compositors, and the dirty jokes shared by the men and women alike. In a few weeks, Watson Jennings Miller IV would be free of all this. The prospect of these thoughts, as he drove home to Riverton, pleased him.

For nearly fifty years, Gabriel Wheeler worked at or lived near Graystone High School. He had been the school's custodian most of those years, forty-two to be exact. Hired during the war, he had stayed on the job until he retired seven years ago.

Gabriel Wheeler figured he held the record for spending more time in the school than any other living person. He knew its secrets, having witnessed many events public and private; the private ones entered by people who thought they were hiding by using the school for their various activities. In addition to having spent more time there, Gabriel, until recently, was the only person to live in the school building before Brooks Sheffield moved in.

Gabriel remembered Brooks as a student, and had known

Brooks' father, the newspaper editor. Gabriel's brother-in-law, Boots Wilson, had worked for Mr. Sheffield back in the early 1960s, and later, Gabriel's sister, Enigma, became cook and housekeeper for the Sheffields after Mrs. Sheffield died. Gabriel had kept his distance from the family because, for one thing, his relationship with his sister was strained and he disliked his brother-in-law, who, like himself, drank too much. Gabriel thought Boots a fancy Dan. Boots dressed smartly and had a strange affection, some said affliction, for his cowboy boots, whence his nickname came.

Aside from his sister and brother-in-law, Gabriel had another reason for avoiding contact with the Sheffield family. In the late 1930s, Gabriel got into a scrape with the law and served some time at the county work farm after cutting a man in a knife fight. Luckily, the man had lived, or Gabriel's four-year sentence would have been extended considerably. Mr. Sheffield had written about the incident and jail sentence in The Herald, and while few people knew or remembered what had happened, Gabriel always feared that one day somebody would hold the jail record up and he would lose his school job. School Superintendent Hobbs, of course, knew about the jail record when he hired Gabriel. He had known Gabriel many years and felt he was hard-working and responsible, exactly the kind of custodian the high school needed.

Gabriel lived in the school several years before he married. Eventually he moved into a small shotgun house two blocks north of the school, behind the baseball park.

During his years as custodian, Gabriel had lurked and watched in the corners and shadows of the school. He lurked not out of prurient curiosity, but simply for self-protection against the likelihood of retribution should he spoil the weekly trysting spot of a young doctor, who was a school board member, and a nurse. They had carried on for several months at the school, every Wednesday night, always darting in the back door with the doctor's key and proceeding to the second floor teacher's lounge and its leather sofa. Quick and efficient, they finished their union in half an hour, then walked directly down the stairs, out the door and to their respective homes, Gabriel assumed.

The young doctor, the nurse and other people used the school as a dark, safe haven in which a love affair would go undiscovered. Gabriel reasoned that white folks were just funny about lovemaking. He held no notions about the school's magnetism for such activity, other than people went there to hide their acts of love.

Nowadays, Gabriel Wheeler had steered clear of Brooks Sheffield for another reason. Several months before Sheffield moved into the school, Sam Warren had come to Gabriel and made him an offer. It meant a considerable amount of money, and in a moment of inebriated weakness he sold his set of master keys to Sam Warren. He regretted this later, but the money did come in handy. He had managed to hold onto one key to a door that gave him entry to the school any time he wanted. He had used this key only once, the morning Louie Basford died. Now, he figured, if anyone questioned him about the master keys, he could say he lost them; no one knew about the one remaining key.

Gabriel got up from his well-worn chair three feet from the small black-and-white TV set that illuminated the room. He crossed the room to a bottle of Canadian whiskey and poured half a glass. He reached into his coveralls and brought out the school key. It was time, he thought, to pay his old friend, Mr. Graystone, a visit.

He shut the door. The TV blared throughout his small house. He shivered as he stepped into the cold night air. Surely by now, he was thinking, Brooks Sheffield would be asleep.

Still, outside his door, he hesitated. Down the street, a white woman walked into the light of a street lamp. Gabriel darted back inside his house and watched as she passed. Farther up the street, a big Cadillac pulled up beside the white woman. As she got in, he noticed she was wearing light clothing, too light for this cold weather.

At Sam Warren's farmhouse, Crystal Durrough cringed in fear at the sight of the pickup truck outside her bedroom window. The night before, visiting Brooks Sheffield, had shattered her normal composure and confidence. Sam Warren fumed over Mr. Sheffield's reluctance to sell the schoolhouse. Sam wanted the man gone and the school left alone. The plan had failed because Mr. Sheffield, as Sam called him, refused to cooperate. And Sam was losing his cool now every time something did not go exactly as he had planned. Old Sam was breaking, slipping, faltering in the head. He heated to a boil.

When she left the schoolhouse, Crystal had walked through the black neighborhood to the north. She was uncomfortable doing this, but Sam had insisted she meet him several blocks away. She had no idea she was safe in her trek from the school as, in the late, chilly hours, Sam had watched her from the moment she exited the building and followed her movement while he rolled along in the big Cadillac a block away, paralleling her course along the rugged, pot-holed streets. When he felt she had not been followed, he had wheeled up beside her. She jumped in and they sped off, hugging the back streets of Riverton's north side, and then going west before cutting a long way back south, toward the farmhouse.

The ride had not been a pleasant one. At first, Sam asked a lot of questions about Brooks Sheffield, then receded into quiet rage that lasted most of the night. Just before they reached the farmhouse, Sam exploded.

"You know, Charlotte said you could convince any man to do anything," Sam had started. "Well, I guess you met your match tonight. Problem is, this is costing me plenty, having him stay where he is, smug in knowing that somebody wants to buy that old school building and he not wanting to sell it...

"Tell you what I ought to do to you, you red-haired little whore. I ought to take you out that old barn out beside the house, just like I did Gracey. You know the one!" Without looking at her, Sam grabbed Crystal's bobbed hair with his right hand and jerked her head back into the headrest, twisting her face toward him.

"Did Charlotte show you Gracey? Huh? Gracey has been to the barn. That old barn is fun town. For me, it's fun town. For you, it's pure hell. In the barn there's a two-by-four board, about three feet long. I trimmed one end for a handle. The other end's for you! I'll tie you up naked to the rusty bedsprings in that old barn.   Then... I'll take the board... And then, then... I'll beat you in the head and ass. Beat your white ass until it's black!"

He laughed, jerking the steering back and forth as the car snaked and careened down the road.

"Beat your head. Take that two-by-four... and... beat your sweet, young, motherfuckin' head..."

Crystal screamed at the threats, at the blinding pain twisting down her back. She clawed at Sam, and he let her go and shoved her into the passenger door.

Then he shut up, to recover or to plan, she wasn't sure. She leaned against car door until they arrived at the farm. Sam got out and went into the house, slammed the door and switched off the outside light. Crystal stayed in the car an hour or so before she dared to enter the house. When she did, Sam was asleep.

The next morning, around seven, Sam came into her bedroom, forced sex with her, then told her to drive his Cadillac to Charlotte's Web, stay there, rest up and keep her mouth shut.

He threw a wad of bills on the bed as he zipped up his pants and walked out.

Crystal was shaken. Nervous after the night before and the rough tumble he had just given her, she pulled the blankets around her and waited for him to leave the house. She heard the door slam minutes after he walked out of the room. She heard the old truck start up. Sam Warren drove off.

She got up, went to the closet, grabbed a suitcase and

packed quickly. All she could think of was to get out of the house and away from Sam Warren as fast as she could. She threw the bag on the bed, tossed in small bottles of makeup and some jewelry she had left on the chest of drawers and was ready to leave when she glanced down at the bedspread. She picked up the wad of bills. They were one-hundreds.

All fifty of them.

Chapter 13 - Tears

Several days passed with no sign of Sam Warren. Dub and Brooks talked by phone several times, and on Saturday morning Dub called to ask Brooks to meet him in Valdosta for dinner that night. He said there was more news on the case and they needed to talk.

It had been an incredible week for Brooks. After the excitement of going to Sam Warren's house, the woman's visit and the confrontation with Watt Miller, his moods had swung widely from the high of tracking down a killer to the disappointment of not finding him, wondering if -- and how -- he might have disappeared. During the low points, Brooks thought about Harriet and Jane and Sara. He needed company. On Saturday morning after Dub's call, he went to Sara's -- his first visit in days.

"Glad you're here," she said, opening the front door. "Come in."

"Sara, I..."

"I missed you. Thought you would call or let me know what's been going on," she said, lovingly, but with obvious regret in her voice. "You had me worried to death. I went to the school, but you never seemed to be there. I called Dub, and he assured me your mind was on helping him out with this investigation. Did he tell you I called?"

"I only talked with Dub briefly this morning, so... no."

"Oh." Sara's eyes turned downward. She was silent, and tears welled up in her eyes, and she looked up at him. "Look here, Brooks. The only way I can say this is... Don't ever do this to me again, dammit! You neglected and ignored me. You cast me aside when I cared about you. I tried... Oh God! I... I tried to help you... and you just go off somewhere. Hell, how'd I even know you were alive until... I talked with Dub.

Oh, shit, don't you know I love you! Don't you care about me! I've already lost everything in life once, and I don't want to lose you!"

She fell into him, sobbing. He led her into the living room and eased her down on the sofa. They sat there, he comforting her and telling her, from the deepest part of his heart that, yes, he loved her very much. Then he let her cry, and he held her close. She slumped against him as the tears flowed, then receded. For a long time, they sat in silence.

"What did you mean," Brooks finally said, "when you said you'd already lost everything?"

Sara turned her head into his shoulder and began to shake as tears came anew.

"Sara, what's wrong?"

She rose up and looked at him through red, wet eyes.

"I never told you. I never told you," she said, shaking her head. "I just couldn't tell you."

"What?"

She wiped her face, and tried to gain some composure.

"I didn't move back here just to go to school. Oh, that's a great diversion, getting a doctorate and starting a new life. Just as if I were going right from college to graduate school... and never got married... and never had a beautiful little boy..."

Brooks offered her his handkerchief. She took it and dabbed her face.

"He was a pretty, curly-haired child. His Daddy loved him to death. Lord, I did, too. Had him playing football when he was six years old, baseball, everything."

"Robby?"

"Yes, Robby. My little Robby." She turned away from him for a moment.

"Sara..."

She put up a hand. "Wait, let me just tell you this. I care about you, and I've got to tell you this."

She turned to him, sitting up on the sofa.

"Robby started at Auburn a year after our divorce. I

stuck it out in Birmingham until he graduated from high school and was into his freshman year. His father and I didn't get along at all at that point. I wasn't sure what I would do, but I already had thought about going back to school. Auburn was my first choice. I guess I was bound and determined to be near my boy.

"That March, Robby and some friends went to Panama City Beach for their spring break. I hadn't seen him in a week or so when he went, but he was going to drive up to Birmingham that weekend to visit me before heading back to school.

"Brooks, I never saw him again. He was killed in a car accident Friday night on the way to Birmingham..."

"Sara, no!"

"He died instantly, with one of his friends."

She broke down again, and Brooks fought back his own shock of the news.

"I had nothing after he was gone. So... I came home. To what always was really home for me."

"Sara. Oh, Sara." Brooks pulled her close and became lost for a time in their closeness, and in their mutual anguish.

"Oh, Sara. Sara, I do love you." He kissed her head as it rested against his shoulder. "I'm so sorry. I'm so terribly sorry."

For Sam Warren, the time had come to implement Phase Two of the Plan. Never mind that Phase One had failed. That was OK, since none of that mattered now. Sam puttered around the barn, at first, as if he had forgotten what he came in to do. Then he seemed to remember and directed himself toward the task at hand. The corner, yes, the corner room where he kept things for the small Ford tractor. Cans of gasoline, several broken cases of oil, a small barrel of grease and sundry tools amid coils of rusty chain, all of which was covered in dust. He mumbled constantly to himself, thinking things out. Had a plan.

She didn't help. Phase one, gone.

He looked down, licking his lower lip and sucking in saliva that drooled from one corner of his mouth as he sought his prize there on the floor of his tool shed. He found exactly what he wanted. Yep, and plenty of it here.

In the weeks since he shot and killed Louie Basford, Sam Warren had walked, at first, a confident, easy path; now, he was running, and his mind stumbled.

He had first realized something was amiss after his second visit to Charlotte's Web, after the shooting. Charlotte had stayed behind, tidying the place before heading to Tallahassee. He'd spotted the dark car parked on the roadside in some palmetto bushes, had made out two people in the car, and wondered why, why in hell, would anyone be parked on a sand road in the woods of north Florida on a Sunday morning.

He thought about the car all the way back to his farm. Who?

Finally, when he felt certain that someone was following him, paranoia set in. It became apparent to Sam Warren that he or Charlotte or both of them, maybe some of her customers, could have been watched for some time. How long this might have been going on, he couldn't imagine.

He stared into the rearview mirror. A few cars, but none real close, dotted the highway along Interstate 10, just east of Tallahassee. Sam slowed to fifty-five, kindergarten speed for him. He punched the cruise control there, sat back and watched. Nothing unusual.

Near Monticello, Florida, he exited for a lone service station and grocery, slowing and keeping his eyes on the rearview. At the top of the exit ramp, he pulled over and observed the traffic below more closely. Several cars moved past, snowbirds mostly, he could tell from the different colors of their license plates, on their way to Jacksonville, Miami, Orlando and Walt Disney World, any number of Florida places. Just down the road, the giant rural interchange connecting Interstate 10, east and west, with Interstate 75, north and south, delivered millions of tourists a year through Georgia and into Florida, then back home to Canada, Michigan, Illinois. Snowbirds mostly.

Sam looked everywhere, keeping his eyes on the cars behind him, and just as he was about to drive over to the grocery, he noticed a dark car had pulled over onto the median, about half-mile back. He hit the brake and stared. A figure was walking from the car to the bushes just off the interstate. Funny, Sam thought, somebody stopping there to whiz, when the exit's right here.

He hit the gas, hung a sharp left onto the road leading over the interstate and headed north toward Monticello. He slowed on the other side of the overpass and saw the figure on the median standing halfway between the car and the bushes, saw him looking toward the overpass and then move briskly back to the car. Sam sped away, cruising at the speed limit to Monticello, heading east on U.S. 90 toward Madison, watching his mirror constantly. Save for a few cars and several farm vehicles, not many people traveled the highway that Sunday morning.

He took his time going home, traveling an out-of-the-way route north to Valdosta, west across the northern part of Piscola County, then back east and south before satisfying himself that no one tailed him home. When he drove up to his house late that evening, Charlotte's little surprise had already arrived. Gracey sat waiting for him in her beat-up Honda Civic.

The next day, having thought over, Sam decided to do some checking around on his own. First, he would call the sheriff's office. Nothing wrong with that, he knew the deputy well. Then he would find out more about that fellow who lived in the school, that newspaper boy from Atlanta. Then he would lay low and retreat back to Florida, somewhere, to relax and think. Think about what he would do next.

By Monday afternoon, he had made some calls, learning the sheriff was at a dead-end without a suspect. Still, he faced the old dilemma: How to run Brooks Sheffield out of

Riverton? Sam knew he'd have to act quickly. At first he thought of using as a way to set Sheffield up, embarrass him, or otherwise hasten his departure. Problem was, when Sam got home, Gracey and a john were partying pretty heavy. She was so high she thought Sam was another customer, but he'd taken care of the situation, had thrown the john out and escorted Gracey out to the barn. That's when Sam tied her to the bedsprings and beat her severely.

With that, Sam started over. He would get one of Charlotte's girls, one he liked for her smarts and cool manner. He would make a special trip to Charlotte's Web and bring back a nicely wrapped surprise gift and proposition for Mr. Brooks Sheffield, known in the neighborhood as the Schoolhouse Man. Damn fool name, Sam laughed to himself.

Yes, indeed, he thought as he bent over to gather the main ingredient for his plan. Mr. Brooks "Schoolhouse Man" Sheffield had another surprise coming. And Sam Warren would deliver it himself this time.

Again Brooks waited at a table in a restaurant -- this time the Pig'n'Plate barbecue in Valdosta -- for Dub Campbell, who was late. The agent walked in, waved and ducked into the men's room.

He walked over to Brooks. "Sorry, I been on the phone to our Florida friends and Sheriff Johnson."

"So, sit down and tell me about it."

Dub turned around and looked around the restaurant. They were in a back booth, and no one sat close to them. Then he leaned over the table.

"Well, Florida's getting ready to make, how shall I say it, a hostile takeover of our old buddy's enterprises in the Sunshine State. That's about that on that."

"And, what else?"

"Hold on to your britches," Sam said, grabbing a menu and waving for the waitress. "I'm hungry."

They ordered their food, and when the waitress left, Dub

leaned forward again.

"Sheriff Johnson made an arrest last night of some local drug dealers. Seems they're your neighbors, right down the street from the schoolhouse."

"Holy..."

"He scared 'em good... about the shooting and all. Treated 'em just like suspects. They caved in pretty quickly from what he tells me. And guess what? Louie Basford had been distributing crack in your 'hood. He'd been the link between Sam Warren's trade and the street traffic for several months."

"So, the shooting was a drug thing, apparently?"

"We don't know that. It's kind of strange, really. You didn't hear anything about drugs before Sam shot Louie?"

"No, nothing. Just what I told you... about the old man accusing Louie of cheating him. Nothing else."

"Louie apparently had been pulling off a few bags for himself. We know he didn't use it. So, he might have been setting some aside and selling it himself, or just plain taking money from Warren, which would have been pretty hard to do, we think. The boys Sheriff Johnson arrested last night confirmed some of this. They said Louie had bragged about his stash of crack and his coming retirement. He, of course, was pretty stupid to be telling this to crack dealers, but he wasn't stupid enough to hint where it was. He did tell one of them he had the crack tucked away in a pile of rags. They said he always laughed at this as if it were a joke, so they weren't sure what to believe. They did say Louie had access to the school, and they saw him in there one or two times late in the evening. You recall anyone breaking in or trying to since you moved in?"

"No, just that one night. Oh, there are always strange sounds in that old place. And hell, some of the doors or windows could be jimmied. It's a big building."

The food arrived, and Dub, uncharacteristically, ignored it to continue.

"Well, I've got a theory, and one I haven't run by the

sheriff. I think Louie put his little retirement plan somewhere in the school."

"Hell! But where?"

"You have a storage room with towels or drapes or something like that piled in it?"

"No, nothing like that. Shoot, that would catch fire quicker than anything. Mostly the things the school board stored there were administrative files, paint, some supplies, that's about all."

Dub dabbled in his barbecue, ate several bites, and told Brooks his plan.

"We need to look around your old schoolhouse, my friend. The quicker, the better."

Brooks was halfway through his meal, but he was ready.

Dub picked up the tab, dropped some change for a tip, and they headed for their cars, choosing to drop Dub's off at his office and take Brooks' car to Riverton.

Across the treetops along the western horizon, now blackened by night, swept a glow over all of Riverton. Clouds hung low, so the glow burned distinctly across a wide area through the darkness. Its exact location could not be determined, but it probably came from the bright lights of the football field at the new county high school. Brooks held the Volvo to around fifty as they rode along the gently rolling farmland. The road dipped down, and for a short while he lost sight of the horizon, but on the next rise the glow was visible again, this time for a considerable distance as the Volvo rolled past cornfields in stubble and through the stench of hog farms.

He could have used a heater in the ancient Volvo, although Dub didn't complain. The coolness of the night reminded him of other nights years ago, out on a date after a football game, searching the back farm roads of Piscola County for a loving spot, shadowy oaks offering solitude and shelter, peace and quiet, for just a little while. Then a thought exploded into his mind, just as if a roman candle rocketed into the night sky, booming, and spraying a thousand colored sparks toward the ground.

"On the rag!"

Dub shot his eyes at the driver. "Huh?"

"On... the... rag. That's it! Get it!" Brooks said.

"Get what?"

"That was Louie's little joke. A bad one, but a joke anyway. A pile of rags. The crack cocaine. There are boxes of sanitary napkins stacked in a small storage room in the teachers' lounge on the second floor of the school. I discovered them last summer when I was poking around up there."

"Holy shit! You may just be right, good buddy. Hit it faster."

"I'd be willing to bet money that was it, if he hid anything in that school."

"Yeah, believe you may be on to something."

The glow on the night sky caught Brooks eye again. His thoughts drifted back, to a night in the chilly, late fall with the old high school band standing on the football field, the crowd shivering and singing "The Star-Spangled Banner." As the last chord squeaked into the cold night, a snare drummer snapped a cadence off the field, cheers rose, the teams jogged in, and the game began.

The lights shone brightly across Riverton those nights. The lights. Tonight. Were shining. Brightly. The football field.

March.

The vision jolted deep inside him. He felt his heart pounding, and he pushed the accelerator into the floorboard, trying to press the car even faster. The engine groaned as the springy speedometer needle lurched to one-twenty. Brooks held this for a moment, before nervously slowing to sixty.

"Dub?"

"Yeah."

"That glow."

"I was thinking the same thing. Go, son. Let's get there."
They both fell into silence.

As they neared Riverton's outer northeast corner, the glow grew much brighter, soon becoming a blaze of flame. At the top of the hill just outside town, he could tell there was something on fire somewhere across town. A fire that consumed something quite large.

No, not likely. It couldn't be. Maybe it was one of the tobacco warehouses or the elementary school or the old, run-down hotel where the Guatemalan families lived? He felt sick, opened the window, shivering in a cold, scary sweat as icy night air rushed into the car. His foot ached as he pressed the Volvo's accelerator to the floor.

He avoided driving through town, taking instead the old toilet-paper road from the north side, which ran straight into town.

At the crest of Bentley Dairy Hill he viewed clearly his worst fear. Straight ahead, the bright orange furnace was exploding skyward.

Dub put his hand on his friend's shoulder.

Sam had parked the truck in an alley behind the field house, well out of sight but close to the school. He wouldn't have far to carry the two cans of gasoline and could get back to the truck fast and away through back streets. He was sure the fire would catch fast, burn long and steady.

He was so right about that. Too right. Sam didn't start at the basement or even on the first floor. Sloshing gasoline and giggling, he lugged the cans up to the second floor, to the spot where he had shot Louie Basford, and the spot where, so many years before, it had happened. When was it, sixty years ago, now, or more? He stopped outside the teachers' lounge, where Sam had been the victim. Where old Mr. Barnes, his teacher, took Sam, the boy, one afternoon after school for punishment. Where the teacher pulled down the boy's britches, touched him, and tried to force the boy to do that

awful, terrible thing. Sam resisted, fighting off Mr. Barnes --
and suffering a severe whipping by the teacher, who left the
boy sobbing beside the leather sofa.

And now, again at the teachers' lounge on the second
floor of Graystone High School, Sam Warren became lost in
the rage and torment of the years, and he did something
really stupid. He set the cans down in the hall, next to the
lounge, and danced up the hall, laughing and hooting.

"You fool! You simple fool!" he shouted to Louie
Basford and went back to the gas cans. There was the
teachers' lounge where, he remembered, he'd raped some girl
on the sofa, couldn't remember who. He picked up one of the
gas cans.

"Just a leettle bit, to scare dat feller off. Yessiree. Mr.
Barnes and Mr. Sheffield. You are cordially invited... Hee
hee hee... to a little... conflagration... in your honor..."

He poured out a puddle of gasoline and, without further
thought or hesitation, struck a match and dropped it in.

He never considered that he stood not more than three
feet from the puddle. The gas cans were closer.

Sam needn't have worried whether it would take one or
two cans of gasoline to ignite the old Graystone High School,
the dearly remembered alma mater to hundreds of Riverton
and Piscola County grads. He needn't worry at all, for at that
moment, all his sins raged up before him in the inferno's
blast. For just that gasp of time, Sam saw the black spot that
was his life.

The exploding cans threw flames up and down the hall
and drenched Sam Warren in fire. He collapsed, screaming
and helplessly batting the flames that engulfed him.

The entire second floor was ablaze and, in minutes, the
flames spread to the first floor and into the basement.

By the time Brooks and Dub arrived, firefighters were
working furiously around the building. As they got out of the
car, the building's north wall caved in, sending more flames
flying high, and the three oak trees close to the building
caught and burned quickly.

Brooks was numb. Stricken, he turned away. There was a man standing next to him, a black man whose face reflected flickers of the raging fire. He looked familiar, Brooks thought, and saw the man's heavy lower lip quiver and tears fall from his eyes.

Gabriel Wheeler cried as he watched the schoolhouse burn to the ground. His schoolhouse. He shook his head and turned to walked away.

Brooks followed. "Mr. Wheeler, isn't it?"

Gabriel looked back, wiping his face on his shirtsleeve.

"Mr. Wheeler," Brooks said again. "You were the janitor here for... how many years?"

Several people had mentioned Gabriel Wheeler to Brooks after he moved into the school. They told him to check with Gabriel if he wanted to know anything, because Gabriel knew the old school better than anybody. Brooks had intended to do this, but he never did, and now he regretted it. He might have consulted him on several things that needed repair, he knew, or at least have invited him over the school. Now it was too late.

Gabriel looked down at the ground. The brightness of the fire cast a shadow of the two men against the Volvo.

"For so many years I been keepin' that old school there. Hard work. Good work, though, that old school." He turned back to the school.

Three fire trucks, one a tanker, were moved back as the firefighters had backed off, the building now gone. A crowd of onlookers was growing larger, some of the curious getting too close. Brooks saw the sheriff's car arriving. Dub had walked over to talk to the fire chief, and they both came over to Brooks and Gabriel.

"You Brooks Sheffield?" the chief asked.

"Yessir."

"Were you in the building when it caught?"

"No sir."

"Who else was in there, you know?"

"No one."

The fire chief looked at Dub, then at Gabriel Wheeler. "You see anyone?"

"They was somebody who went in there," Gabriel said softly.

"Who, man, why in hell didn't you get us before? It's gone up, and anyone who was in there is dead by now."

"Well, he might have left," Gabriel said, knowing Sam Warren had not left the building, knowing the old man had died inside.

"There's more than a body going up in that smoke," Dub said. "A whole lot more."

The fire chief, frustrated about Gabriel's statement and perplexed at what Dub said, hurried over to Sheriff Johnson, who was standing next to his cruiser talking with the mayor. The sheriff came toward Brooks and Gabriel, motioning a deputy to follow, and Gabriel nervously retreated a step. Brooks took him by the arm. "Don't worry," he told him. "I know what happened. Tell them what you know. You'll be OK." Then he looked at Dub. "We can help him?" Dub nodded.

Gabriel looked more concerned than ever, but he talked to the sheriff and Dub, telling them he saw Sam Warren's truck -- he pointed it out to them -- at the school shortly before the fire started. He said he figured Warren was inside when he saw the truck. He said he had seen Warren around the school a couple of days ago and even before that. He stopped short of mentioning the night of the shooting.

"Well if he or anybody else is in there, they are gone now," said Sheriff Johnson. He looked at Dub. "Campbell, you'd better get your crime lab people and tell them to get on down here." Then the sheriff sniffed and walked away.

The fire chief had seemed ready to ask Gabriel more questions, but he just walked off as Dub intervened. The chief turned back to the biggest fire he had managed in years. Now he was more concerned with crowd control. People do get too close, he had said. Dub left to make his call.

Brooks and Gabriel watched the last walls crumble, then

fall in. He wanted to console him, this man, but he couldn't share his disappointment and grief with anyone, nor did he want to intrude.

"You did a real good job," he said to Gabriel, extending his hand. Gabriel looked at him, without smiling, and shook hands.

"Yessir, I did."

With no thought of offering Dub a ride home, Brooks got into the Volvo, started it up, looked at the fire once more, and drove away. He went to Houston Avenue to see Sara and tell her again how much he loved her.

Epilogue

Brooks Sheffield stood as he spread out several newspapers on the roll top desk. He picked up The Riverton Herald's latest edition, Thursday, March 19, 1989.

The front-page story, like the various accounts in other newspapers on the desk, reported on the prostitution ring, along with some illegal drug distribution, in several Florida cities masterminded by the late Sam Warren, a Riverton businessman. The Herald had just been printed, and its story, while several days behind the dailies, offered a perspective the others missed.

All the stories told of the hundreds of thousands of dollars being made by the ring, which had operated in Tallahassee, Jacksonville and elsewhere in Florida, but The Herald's account related a great deal about Warren's history in the town and the local law officers who worked on the investigation.

Brooks read how GBI Agent W.D. Campbell, working with Piscola County Sheriff Carroll Johnson, helped Florida law officers track down the ring's leaders.

The week before, officers arrested Charlotte Welles in Tallahassee and charged her with racketeering, prostitution and deriving support from prostitution.

The stories detailed her arrest, how the six-month investigation had proceeded and listed numerous others involved in or charged in the case. Although providing no names, the story hinted of lists of the ring's customers, including well-known businessmen and legislators. In all, more than 100 prostitutes worked in the ring, by far the biggest ever broken up in Florida. If convicted, Charlotte Welles would go to prison for years, the estimated length of sentence varying from one newspaper account to another.

Brooks finished the story, folded the paper neatly and placed the copy of The Herald on top of the others.

He sat down at the desk. His hurt over the last weeks, months and years had eased. He felt a healing, a wholeness about himself. But every so often he had also heard a rumble, something deep inside, calling out to him. Come back, the inner voice echoed, come back to a finer place and time. Come back to your past. The echo died, and he glanced, with arms resting on the chair, through window blinds and onto the side street of his hometown. His eyes focused on nothing in particular. He just looked, and as he did, he thought about the task before him, the challenge in the next week and the months to come.

This challenge was pulling him from despair, and pushing him forth. He thought about a lot of matters that needed attention, community concerns that in recent years in Riverton had been ignored. He thought about what arose from the school's ashes. Insurance money from the fire would help build a community center for the neighborhood surrounding the property and a job-training site for the entire town. The rest of the money would be channeled into his own dream, a legacy diminished of late, but one being reborn now.

As he contemplated these things, his mind's eye beheld the image of Sara Compton, the woman he needed so badly the night the school burned and the woman who waited for him, even as she dived into her final busy months of finishing her doctorate. She couldn't seem to give enough of herself, he thought, and he owed her so much. He concluded that, indeed, he had accomplished something in returning to Riverton. He had recaptured an important part of his past, a past whose small voice still called to him. His friends shaped the best part of this.

The Schoolhouse Man glanced down again at the papers

arranged on the desk in front of him. The Riverton Herald, under new management, proclaimed in a banner headline that week: "Deceased Riverton Man Headed Florida Prostitution Ring."

He smiled at the next line of type: "By Brooks Sheffield, Editor."

The End

CPSIA information can be obtained
at www.ICGtesting.com
Printed in the USA
LVHW080059131120
671598LV00018B/888

9 781524 258313